I never looked back.

Left that place, left the buildings and the field, left Waller dying in the dirt and the white women in the house and never once looked back. The other slaves—no, free people—would have to take care of themselves now. Bluecoats coming, bringing freedom to everyone, sweeping clean all the dirt there was, but I didn't look back.

Had to find my children.

GARY PAULSEN

Sarny

A Life Remembered

LAUREL-LEAF BOOKS

Published by
Bantam Doubleday Dell Books for Young Readers
a division of
Random House, Inc.
1540 Broadway
New York, New York 10036

Visit us on the Web! www.randomhouse.com

Educators and librarians, for a variety of teaching tools, visit us at
www.randomhouse.com/teachers

ISBN 0-440-21973-6

RL: 4.3

Reprinted by arrangement with Delacorte Press

Printed in the United States of America

September 1999

10

OPM

Also for Sally Hemings

Beginning words, 1930

It's quiet now, so quiet sometimes it seems like everything is covered with layers of soft dust so thick the sound can't come through. Must have been fifteen, no, sixteen years since I could hear much more than a hum. Back when I was my Biblical age limit. Eighty years old.

I am ninety now, ninety and just exactly four. I've been in this home must be fourteen years waiting for something. I'm not sure what it is I'm waiting for. Maybe to die and to go see Delie and Nightjohn again because I get to missing them more now that I'm getting on. Not old, now—just getting on. I learned that when I was twenty and eight—how not to say old when speaking of a lady. Just getting on. Woman taught me that had the name of Miss Laura and she lived in a fancy house in New Orleans where men came and went. I

1

cleaned the house and helped her when I was there after my children. Before she passed on she told me so many things I'm still digging them out of my thoughts like parsnips left in the ground all winter and dug up fresh in the spring.

Once a week a doctor he comes into my room and he looks and he smiles and he pokes here and pokes there and says something to me. I smile at him and nod and he nods back and leaves me for another week and I don't have a single idea of what he says but it don't matter. He's young and he means to help and what he says don't count as much as how he gets to saying it. I know he cares and that's all that signifies.

I like that word. Signifies. I've used it a lot, what with living and all. When I married the first time I said to him, "Martin, this marriage signifies that we're bound for life." And he agreed, though I'm certain as day that he didn't know what the word meant until later when I told him. And he meant it because even though we were still slaves he married me with a minister with our heads in the big bowl and he was my only until they worked him to death. My first husband. Died when he was twenty and seven. Worked down and broke and died just two years before Lincoln's war it made us free.

Sometimes I miss Martin too. Big hands, deep laugh. Once I saw him laugh so hard he slammed his hand down on a cast-iron stove lid and broke it. But gentle. Oh my, so gentle. He could pull a splinter out of my finger and I didn't even feel it and there were other times when he would pick me up just like I was a feather and . . . well, no mind to that. Not in somebody ninety and four years old. Been sixty years, well, forty truth be told, since I thought of any man lifting me like a feather. Shame *on* me for thinking about it now. Well, not too much shame. The brain don't know it gets old. That Miss Laura she told me about that—said a grandmother's body has the same brain as a young girl. Body gets old but the brain won't admit it and there you be groaning and bending and making old sounds when you get up and you look in the mirror and your brain won't let you see you're old. Just be a young thing looking back at you and you put a little on this wrinkle and a little on that and forget you're sixty and three. Try to be twenty and seven in your mind.

Don't get me started on that, getting old. I've seen too much, done too much to feel old. Old is for them that sits and I never could be one to sit.

I tried to explain things to the nice young girl that wheels me out into the sun of an afternoon. She couldn't be a day over forty and three. But she smiles like the doctor smiles and cares and nods and we just stay in our own worlds.

She's the same girl that changes the flowers of a week. I think she picks them out on the grounds because I've seen holes in the flower beds but Lord, they smell so sweet I don't care are they stolen. Just about everything else on me is worn and broke down but my nose still works and what the smell of flowers can do for the little girl in my brain would make you dance to see it.

It's not bad here. You have to wait somewhere when you're looking to go visit old friends and it's warm here outside Dallas, especially when the sun comes in the white windows on the east side over my bed. 'Course I'm working all the time, working on my memories and of a time my grandson Carlisle who was from Tyler comes by. He's fifty and four though it don't seem possible that a person still drawing breath can have a grandson fifty and four and I don't think I've seen him in over a year, maybe a year and a month.

It was him to tell me to write some of this down. "Write it all down," he said. "Much as you can know. Someday people will want to read it, read it all." Sounded like Nightjohn, all over again, and so I do. The girl who does the flowers brings me notebooks and a pencil and I've been writing all this year when my fingers ain't stiff and lazy. Got me a pile of pages, must be thicker than two fists. I was always one to talk a lot and I guess it just comes into the writing the same as speaking.

Ain't that something? That a sprite everybody looked right over, clean over the top when they were busy to see something, would be the one to live and live and write it all down.

Ain't that something?

The
Plantation

O N E

The reading didn't spread so fast at first.

Took on to be slow, like watching spilled molasses smearing across a table. Nightjohn he was gone but I got to where the letters meant more all the time and pretty soon I was working words with two and even three parts in them, writing whole sentences helping others and before too long some were doing the same.

Women at first, because they had the time and some kind of toughness so they could learn at night even after working in the day. Men a little slower. They worked until they dropped, busted and sore and didn't have much left for learning, but they did just the same, only slower.

Came a day maybe a year after Nightjohn he was gone, came a day when it changed. One day it seemed people were having trouble with the words and some would stammer at them and make them slow and with thick sounds and the next day it was different. Seemed everybody was reading and then it spread, oh my yes, it spread like a fire in dry grass.

One would help two and two would help four and nearly everybody came to know reading and writing and then it went to other plantations and they tried to stop it.

The men with whips and dogs they tried to stop it because they knew, they knew what it meant. Meant we were learning, coming to know how it was other places, other times.

Places and times where there weren't slaves, where one didn't own another, couldn't own another by law. And then, some who read and some who didn't, but just listened to the ones who read, some started to run. Run north.

Running was the same as reading. It started slow, like molasses at first. They'd run and get caught, get whipped, get cut, get hung sometimes, get killed sometimes.

But they kept running, trying it, because they knew from reading could they stay with it, follow the drinking gourd, the Big Dipper, and get north, get away, they could be free. Free to read what they wanted to read, know what they wanted to know, free to be more.

I would have run. As sure as I took a breath I would have run and there wasn't a thing in the world that could have kept me from running except being a woman caught me from the side.

One day I was a girl, doing girl things, and then another year had gone and another. Must have been three years since Nightjohn he left, and I wasn't a girl anymore.

Was a woman.

With woman's thoughts and woman's doings. 'Course others noticed it. Waller he noticed it and wanted me to be with men but Nightjohn he took it out of Waller some way. Oh, Waller he was still mean, mean as snakes, and he used the whip and his hands in bad ways but there was something gone from the center of him, some of the hardness. Got to where it was easy to get around him and when he would tell me to do something with men I would nod and then talk to the men and we would just let on there was doings but there wasn't. Wasn't any doings at all.

But I was changed now and part of me was all turned around. Of an afternoon I was sitting shucking dry corn for the crib, a late summer afternoon and Martin he walked by and he filled my eyes like I was seeing him for the first time.

I knew him when I was a baby, saw him all along and didn't notice him and now it was like an ox hit with the hammer.

Martin I thought—my, my, look at Martin.

Look at *all* of Martin. And I did, looked right at him and smiled with my chin down and my eyes open so shameless old Delie she saw it and called me a little hussy. Didn't matter because Martin he looked right back at me and smiled and from then on we didn't need words except I wouldn't do women's doings until we married.

So we put our heads in the big kettle to make it right and married with a Bible under our hands, a Bible I could read some of, most of, and we took a blanket together and he was my husband and I was his wife and so I couldn't run.

We talked on it some. On the blanket after a month and two and three we talked at nights alone of running because others had run and some made it.

But before long I was going to mother and Delie she held the string and needle up and said it would be a boy, a strong boy, but that I'd have a hard birthing the first time.

First time, I thought. Like there was going to be more but I didn't say anything. I was showing some and Waller he let me to slow down a bit because he had heard about the needle test and knew Delie was 'most always right and a boy would make a man and a man would make him money.

The house people found a piece of paper

wrapped around hard sugar once that was a bill of sale for selling a man slave. He fetched twelve hundred and fifty dollars at the auction—that's more money than a free man made in four years working a good job. More money than a slave made in four lifetimes. That's what Waller saw. He saw me showing and it meant money to him. Martin he talked more about running. But I couldn't.

I would have lost the baby, did we run, and so we stayed, me because I had to and Martin because he was good to the core of him and wouldn't leave me and it was a shame because it killed him, staying on to work. Waller he worked him to death in three more years. Martin he was some older than me and Waller started him to working heavy, lifting and pushing heavy things, trying to move cotton bales bigger than ten men, and it finally killed him. Something broke inside and he bled and died in one night.

But not at first. At first we got to have some living.

The baby came and Delie she was right. It was a hard birth but a strong boy and we named him Tyler because I saw the name on a bill of lading and thought it was pretty and sounded like a good name for a strong boy and Martin he agreed.

We talked of running again but it was hard

to run with a baby and by the time Tyler was old enough to understand being quiet and hiding at night I was with child again and so we couldn't run.

Delie she said this time it would be a girl with an easy birth. Martin he only lived another year. Saw the baby come—we named her Delie—and then came a dark time, so dark even remembering it hurts.

Martin he died one day. Was a sunny day and I wanted it to be gray, raining, wanted the sky to cry because Martin died. I couldn't stand it. Breath didn't come, couldn't see, even forgot the children. Just sat in a corner of the slave quarters and hated. Hated Waller, hated cotton, hated God for taking him, for making Waller, for making cotton, hated everything while Martin he died broke inside.

Delie she sat with me, held me, cried with me and patted me on the side of my head and wiped my cheeks.

"It will be all right," she said. "Everything will be all right."

"No," I said. "It won't. Nothing's all right with Martin gone."

And it wasn't, not then, not ever.

Worse came then. I didn't think there could be anything worse than Martin dying but worse came. Delie she died from being old. I was with her when it happened. We were working on leather, softening mulehide to be made into harness traces, and Delie she said to me, "I believe I'd better sit a spell," and she went over by the side of the quarters and sat and closed her eyes. I brought her water in the metal dipper and said her name.

"Delie?"

But she was gone, dead and gone just as quiet as going to sleep and we buried her in the slave ground up by the hill and I didn't seem to be able to see over it. First Martin and then Delie. Was like a wall around me and hadn't it been for little Delie and Tyler I think I would have passed from a broken heart. But it wasn't over. The dark times.

Waller he took to drinking and gambling.

It started slow. Some of the house slaves saw it first, that he was playing cards in town and coming home late after we were asleep in the quarters and sitting with whiskey until he passed out. Time was Waller he had power over people, even other white people, and he grew on the power, fed on it, but all that left him now. Old woman said to me, "Man takes a drink, drink takes a drink, drink takes a man." Didn't take Waller long to go through it all. Everything in him that had power in it left him. He was still mean, but it didn't work out of him like it did once and some of the slaves would point at him when he was drunk and smile behind their hands. I would have felt bad for the white women in the house didn't I hate them so. But in their own little ways they were as mean as he was and inside my heart I was glad Waller was falling apart. It was stupid because I didn't see what this would mean for us. We belonged to Waller, just like mules or cotton. Just property. All of us, even little Delie and Tyler.

And soon enough Waller he couldn't do anything but lose.

Time passed, and more time until both the babies were weaned and running in shirt-waists. Been others to see me, other men, but the memory of Martin was too sharp, cut like a knife, and I didn't see the other men. Would I try to look at them I'd just see Martin, Martin's smile, the way he moved, his strong hands, and I'd turn away.

It was then the year eighteen hundred and sixty-one. I was a full woman aged twenty and four with my two children growing up my legs, both starting to work, and we started in to hearing things.

Was a rumble up north, we heard, a rumble that there would be a war, and then there was a war. We found some newspapers and we could read now, most of us, read as fast as our eyes could move, and there were stories in the paper about the war and how the North was going to come down and free the slaves.

Didn't say it that way. Not then. Not in any paper in the South where they still used ugly words, bad words for people in the quarters. Didn't say free the slaves. Said the war was to make the Southern states come into line with the North and that emancipation was a part of the fighting. But it was the same—meant to free us and we all prayed with our heads in the pot and I took my children and went to Delie's grave and told her time and again, I said, "They're coming down here, the Northern army is coming to set us free."

And we waited.

And we waited some more and nothing much seemed to be happening. We got papers now and again, wrapped around packages from town, and once a whole newspaper that Billy he stole off a wagon when nobody was looking.

The paper talked of fine things for the South and how well it was going and how they were winning all the battles and it made us all feel sour and down but then I remembered that writing was just people talking on paper. Except for in the Bible, could a person lie when he talked, he could lie when he wrote. I sat in the quarters of a night with a candle taken from the big house under a blanket with little Delie and Tyler holding the blanket off the flame and read the paper again. Read not what it said in words but what it said in thoughts.

Words were bad. Battles were going fine, it said, Confederacy winning wherever it fought, it said, big battle at a place called Gettysburg up in a North state named Pennsylvania. Said the Confederate states won a "resounding victory." All that it said in words.

But there were more words than those. Words in the back, two solid pages of names of the Confederate dead who died at Gettysburg in the fighting. Small print, names on top of names on top of names, each one a dead soldier and I don't know nothing of battles and how they fought wars but I knew you didn't win battles by having all those names of dead men. That's how you lost battles, and lost wars, and I felt good. Not for the dead names. Might I hate them, every one was still some mother's child and I felt bad for the mothers. But Lord it was good to think the North was winning.

More words. Talked of how there wasn't any more sugar, how people couldn't ship cotton because of Northern ships closing harbors, how flour was getting on to being four and five dollars a pound in the city. People winning wars don't be paying five dollars a pound for flour—that comes from losing.

So I told the rest that it was nigh over and that could we just hang on, hang on, soon we would be free when the North won the war.

Except Waller he got more drunk and lost more and more playing cards in the town and one day he came out with another man.

Tall man, greasy face narrow like a hand ax. Had a transport wagon with rings bolted in the floor boards to old chains. For transporting people. For moving slaves.

But it came empty. Waller he wasn't buying slaves.

He was selling. Found later he had lost and lost more at cards with no money left and all he had to sell was slaves.

Had us to sell.

We all knew it was coming and we all hid in the quarters or in the barns or in the bushes thinking couldn't he see us he wouldn't think to sell us, crazy thinking. He took Billy for the wagon and another man named Tuck who had been watching me and I had looked at a time or two. And then Waller he found me in the quarters and took little Delie and Tyler and bolted them in the wagon.

"No!" I screamed it and he turned from

the wagon and hit me once with the whip, not to mark just to get my attention but I didn't care.

Couldn't take my children.

Sweet things, my heart, part of Martin part of me things, sweet little darling things that were all my soul and breath and what I lived for, all my memories and all my thoughts were little Delie and Tyler and that low man he chained them into the wagon with the two men.

"They'll fetch good," he said to the man driving the wagon. "Those two pups. They'll bring good . . ."

I ran to the wagon and said things, wild things, said I would do anything for him only please don't take my children, not my heart, not all of me, not that.

But he paid me no more mind than he'd pay a braying mule and when the wagon left I started to run after it but he grabbed me and dragged me back and put a shackle on my wrist and tied me to the same chains on the wall where they tied Delie to whip her.

I watched the wagon, pulled at the chains and watched the wagon until it went around some trees and I couldn't see it, and then I listened to the squeak of the wheels and the rattle of the chain until I couldn't hear it and then I listened to the memory of the wagon in my mind, every sound, every sight of it until it was dark and somebody brought me some corn bread and a piece of pork fat.

First I didn't eat. First I just squatted against the wall bound tight by chains and had dark thoughts, thoughts of what I would do to Waller when I got loose. Kill him, cut him, use an ax on him and then go for my children.

But the thoughts wouldn't work just like starving wouldn't work. I had to be strong I knew and get away not to kill Waller but to find them, find my children, and Waller he would just have to look for his own death.

TWO

It wasn't but six days coming. Happened right in front of me and didn't I know that God was all forgiving and sweet I would think he had a hand in it.

Waller he knew me and knew I would run as soon as he took me off the chain so he didn't let me loose. They brought me food and water and a girl named Lucy she brought me a blanket to sleep in and cover myself for privacy when there was a need.

I worked at the chain, saved pork fat to grease my wrist so it would slip off, but it was too tight and just cut in until I had a sore. Decided to use my brain, started thinking did I act better, didn't fight it, maybe Waller would take me off the chain and I could run but it didn't matter.

There came a day when I was still on the chain and I heard a rumble, like thunder, except there were no clouds in the sky. There are some who believed in evil hants. Not me because I had started to read the Bible and was on my second time through. Had me a Bible left me by old Delie and I never asked where she got it. So I didn't think on hants except this one was full of meaning. Thunder in a clear sky meant big change was coming and I sat a mite thinking on what change it could be when Waller he came out of the house.

Had a gun in his hand, that evil little pistol he loved so much. He looked white, whiter than usual and scared, and he came running towards the barn pointing at something and when I stood to look I saw men running towards the plantation across the north field.

They were wearing blue. Wasn't thunder we heard but guns, big guns far off.

There must have been thirty or forty of them. They were carrying guns, long rifles with bayonets, and Waller he stood by the corner of the barn, stood by me with that silly little pistol in his silly little hand looking at the soldiers come a running and made the last mistake of his sorry mistaken life.

He raised that pistol like he was going to shoot at the soldiers.

Some stopped to shoot at Waller and the bullets missed him and hit the wall, chipped wood and whined away, but so close I crouched down on one knee and a boy came running around the corner of the building.

No more than a boy. Couldn't have been sixteen, seventeen years old. White boy wearing blue pants and a blue jacket that were too big for him and had a rifle 'most as tall as he was with a bayonet on the end.

I saw it all. Slow, it happened. Waller he had the little pistol and the boy he ran around the corner and the bayonet went into Waller. Slick, like Waller wanted it to happen, like he pushed against it. The bayonet it slid into him just above his belt buckle, slid in and came out the back, and the boy he looked surprised, surprised and mean at the same time, so that he pushed harder and lifted Waller a bit, lifted him up and back and then dropped him.

Waller he wasn't dead yet but knew he was dying and I knew it too and the boy he looked at me.

"Please," I said. "Please. He has the key to the shackles in his front pocket. Please."

I didn't think he would do it. He was looking for others to shoot, others to stick, but he kneeled down next to Waller. Waller still looking at his belly where the hole was, holding his hand there to stop it some way, knowing he was going to die he looked at me and then back at his belly while the boy found the key and handed it to me.

"Here," he said. "You're free now—on your own."

"Thank you." He meant free of the chain but I took it for the long road, free now, free. We were all free. Could walk where we wanted to walk, be where we wanted to be.

Free.

I didn't stand long. There were those who stood, looking, wondering. I saw them later. Those who had used the chains for bracing, leaned against slavery to give them strength. Suddenly the brace was gone and some stood, wondering where to turn, how to live.

But I had my children.

Waller he was still alive. Down on his side holding his hands over his belly, his head turned up, and I put my knees down next to him.

"My children," I said. "Where did they go? Where did you send little Delie and Tyler?"

But he didn't answer. Just looked up at me and then down at his stomach and back up and I saw the power go out of him, saw the life go out of his eyes and knew he wouldn't tell me anything.

Just had to move then. Couldn't stay, couldn't wait—had to get moving and keep moving. I went by the quarters and saw Lucy standing by the door and she said, "What am I going to do?"

"Do?" I almost yelled at her. "Why Lord, Lucy, you can do anything you *want*—that's what you can *do.*"

I found an old tow sack by a blanket, threw my other shift in it, a small bag with my needles and thread, half a pan of corn bread that was still in the pan and a pound or so of pork fat. Wasn't much but more than some, more than many had, and it would have to take me to the next food. Would have to take me towards my children.

I never looked back.

Left that place, left the buildings and the fields, left Waller dying in the dirt and the white women in the house and never once looked back. The other slaves—no, free people—would have to take care of themselves now. Bluecoats coming, bringing freedom to everyone, sweeping clean all the dirt there was, but I didn't look back.

Had to find my children.

THREE

I had never seen the town. Had heard of it, talk all the time of all the houses and people and stores. Some of the men went now and again to help load and they came back with stories of men in frock coats and women in long dresses and carriages so fancy it seemed you could eat them. Billy he said he saw a black man eating hard candy from a sack. I had never even seen hard candy let alone eat of it and he said they had it in the stores and would sell it from jars a penny a bag but Billy now and again saw hants and heard whispers others didn't hear so I didn't believe everything he went on about.

The ax-faced man with the wagon had come from the road to town and had taken my children down that road and that's the way I went. Couldn't help but nearly run. They'd been gone six—no, seven—days and maybe they were in that town and I could find them there and my feet they just wouldn't walk slow.

Still I hadn't walk-trotted a mile when Lucy she caught up with me. Tall girl, leggy so she could move, sixteen, seventeen years old with a smile all the time even when things weren't funny. Sometimes she made me think of myself when I was younger though maybe she was a bit smarter and a good bit prettier. Didn't show the smart but it was there.

"Decided to come with you. That's what I *wanted* to do," she said when she caught up. "Except I didn't know you'd be running. It like to killed me catching up."

"They took my children," I said. "I can't walk slow—"

"I know. I was there. Don't you worry, we'll find little Delie and Tyler. Don't you worry." And there was that smile. "Waller he was still laying there when I left."

"I don't care a snip about Waller."

"It's good he's dead."

"I don't care."

"Maybe the pigs will eat him."

I didn't say anything more about him and never did say another word on him until I was old and even now could I see him, Bible or no, I wouldn't forgive him. Spit on his grave.

I didn't know how far it was to town but Lucy had heard it from Billy. "Seven miles," she said. "A mile is the same distance as the length of that south cotton field. So it would be seven of those fields. I figure we've walked three fields so there be four more. To town."

She was carrying a sack that was heavier than mine, big weight down in the bottom. "What's in the sack?"

Her smile widened, seemed to cover her whole face. "Got me an extra shift in there."

"Heavy shift."

"I stopped by the smokehouse on my way out and took two hams. They ain't big but they looked done and I figured we earned them."

"We earned everything—"

"Riders." There was the sound of hooves.

Hard word. Riders. Them that run and come back talk about riders. Men on horses. Hard men. Mean to the bone men with guns and whips and chains and dogs. Riders is the word for the hard men.

But it's wrong this time. These riders are wearing blue, brass buttons glinting in the sun, rattle of sabers and creak of saddles. There were twelve of them, two by twos with a man in charge, an officer, out to the side and a little ahead.

We moved off the road to let them by but they stopped. Officer first, then all the men, stopped and looked down on us.

"You're free now." The officer brushed at a fly that had been following the horses and buzzed his face.

"I know. Yes sir. Thank you. The soldier at the plantation told us that—"

"But there are still dangers. We are just an advanced unit. There are bands of renegade scavengers—rebel deserters—that we haven't rounded up yet, killing and looting."

New word. Scavenger. Didn't know it. But knew the others—killing, looting. "Yes sir."

"You might want to find a safe place to be until things settle down. Look for some Union troops encamped and stay close to them."

"I can't. I've got children to find."

He had been looking away and he looked down on me now. Tall horse, tall man, looked down and smiled like he was a father. "Stay away from people on the roads unless they are soldiers."

"Yes sir."

And they were gone, the horses trotting past. Some of them looked at Lucy and some looked at me and their looks weren't as soft as the officer's. Looking at our shifts, way we stood. Two looked back as they rode away and I thought the officer was right, might be dangerous along the road especially at night. And from more than scavengers. But I didn't say anything and when I turned I saw Lucy and she was smiling back at the men and I thought, too much tooth in *that* smile. Might as well light a lantern and hang it over the store.

"Let's go."

It was afternoon, hot and muggy, and I kept moving and had there been time it would have been a marvel to see the country we traveled through.

Must have been a plantation every mile. Some of them nicer than the one I'd lived on and most of them less and all of them in smoke. Some big houses burning, some barns, sheds. Quarters burning all over the place. Blue-coated soldiers were everywhere. Moving this way and that. All seemed to have a reason to move, a place to get to, a place to leave. A lot of busy work.

Didn't see any gray soldiers except dead ones. Saw a group in a ditch, almost in a row, must have fallen like they stood. All their coats were open to show their bellies and some of them had big holes, some weren't marked so you could see it but they were all dead. Didn't see any dead blue ones, only gray.

Lucy she made the hex sign when we passed the bodies, little and first finger out and thumb down but I shook my head. "They won't bother you. Not now."

"They got spirits," she said. "They all got spirits can come back and hant us."

I didn't think so. They just looked like busted dolls to me but I didn't say anything more about it. Lucy she wanted to make the hex sign it didn't hurt anything and maybe it would help.

Black folks around every corner, over every rise. Some walked with the blue soldiers, following them, smiling but scared-looking like they thought it wouldn't last. Like you could be free and then not free. Not me, I thought, you try to turn me back into a slave and you've got your hands full. Might as well try to turn sawdust back into a tree.

Others they just looked dazed. Didn't know where to go, how to get there. Some followed us for a spell and I looked back once to see six or seven trotting behind us but we set too pushy a pace and they all fell away.

Every one I see, every single one I asked about little Delie and Tyler. Every soldier and every black person and they all try, think hard and try, but none remember seeing them, not even the wagon and the ax-faced man.

Town wasn't like they said. We came to the edge of it in the evening, just as the light was changing and it was getting hard to see. Part of it was light but most of it was smoke. Some buildings were all burned down, some were still burning. I didn't see any fancy carriages or hard candy or pretty dresses or frock coats.

Nothing but ruin. There were no men, no black men, no white men. Some women were there, white women except with all the soot on them they looked black and I stopped one of them on the outskirts. Woman maybe forty, looked sixty, seventy, kept picking at her dress.

"Could you tell me where they take slave children?" I asked. "To sell them?"

But she didn't answer, just looked past me, past Lucy at where a building used to be and there wasn't anything but burned boards and smoke. "We had a store there. We had a store right there. See? Right there where—"

"I had two children, miss," I said. "They came here on a wagon. They must have come here. They were this high, to my waist and a bit more. A girl and a boy. Did you see them?"

Didn't say anything for the longest time. Just kept picking at her dress where there was a hole as big as her hand burned through. I started to turn.

"I had a boy," she said. "I had a son and he went to Antietam and is buried there. I had a son and a store and a husband who ran off and now they're all gone."

"I'm sorry but—"

"I never had slaves. I didn't like slavery. Why did they burn my store?"

"I don't know."

She picked some more, tears cutting the soot on her face, making white streams. "The man you want is Greerson. He owns—I guess owned would be the right way to say it now. He owned the slave yards at the south end of town."

"Thin man, face sharp like an ax, slick hair?"

She nodded. "Yes. He might know what happened to your children. Just go to the south end of town and look for the yards. If you see my husband would you send him home?"

But we were already gone, headed through the broken town, me with my small sack and Lucy with her two hams, looking for the slave yards.

FOUR

We found the yards and almost got to Greerson in time. Yards were pens with slat-board
roofs on them, rings in the wooden walls for
chains, chutes that came out to a central open
area like there was on the plantation for working with the pigs and cattle.

Same as that. There was some smoke where
somebody had tried to fire the pens but the
wood wasn't close enough to burn and it went
out. The place was empty.

Or almost.

Out front of a small shack was the wagon
with the chain rings in it, the wagon that took
my children, and I felt the pull of it, felt that it
had been close to little Delie and Tyler and
thought maybe they were inside the shack but
no, nothing there but papers thrown all over,
boxes of papers.

"Oh Lord," I said. "They're not here."

There was a sound from the back then.
Sound like a hammer hitting meat to soften it

and I ran out around the shack into the main yard opening and there was Greerson.

Not alone though. There was a black man there, big man, hands like my Martin had, shoulders like a door, and he was holding Greerson up against the side fence with one hand and beating him with the other.

Didn't look even mad, the black man. Just as cool were he at a job of work. Hold him with one hand, bring the other back like a club, like a hammer, like a cleaver.

Chunk!

In the forehead, in the face, slow hits that seemed to float, but each time Greerson's head snapped back like a mule had kicked him and I forgot for a moment why I was there. Just watched. Then I thought, no, not yet, I need this man.

"Hold!" I said. "Wait. This man took my children and I need him to tell me where they are."

The black man turned and looked at me. "He laid a whip on me. Laid a whip on all of us, but he laid it on me hard. I'm just taking it back. But I can finish later."

He stood to the side but kept holding Greerson up against the fence by the neck. Greerson he just hung there and when I came close I could see that he wasn't going to be doing any talking. His face looked like a wagon had run over it and both his eyes had rolled back to just show white and what breath there was came in little jerks.

"Greerson—can you hear me? You remember coming for my children? Out to the Waller place? You remember that?" But he didn't hear me, didn't hear anything. "You hit him too hard. He ain't there anymore."

"I'm sorry," the black man said, and he looked sorry too. "I didn't know you were coming or I would have held back a tad."

It was Lucy that saved me. I turned away and the black man went back to hitting Greerson and I moved out of the yard and was near crying, thinking of little Delie and Tyler. The wind blew four ways and they could have gone any of them. No way to know.

"In the shack," Lucy said. "There might be something in all those papers about little Delie and Tyler . . ."

And I would have walked away hadn't she said it, would have walked away and never thought of it, never known.

We went inside and started to work. I didn't know what to look for, didn't know where to begin, but Lucy just picked up a piece of paper and went to reading.

"Male, teeth show age not over eighteen, answers to name of Herman, no whip scars, to be at auction. Nope." She threw it aside and picked up another. "Female, teeth show age between twenty-five and thirty, answers to name of Betty, no whip scars, trained for house duties, to be at auction. Nope."

That's what all the papers were. Bills of sale, hundreds and hundreds of them, all records that Greerson kept for all the time he sold slaves.

It was soon dark, too dark to read, but Lucy she found an oil lamp with an unbroken chimney and some matches and soon we had light. Still hard to read but by holding the paper close to the lamp we could make out the letters.

Must have read fifty or a hundred of them when I looked up and Lucy she was sitting there crying, holding the paper.

"What's the matter?"

"I just come across old Willy. You remember him?"

For certain I remembered him. Delie she said that she and old Willy once had eyes for one another. Soft old man used to carve willow whistles for the children in the quarters. Called them whoop-te-do whistles. Gray hair, gray beard, soft voice, soft smile.

"They sold him for fifty dollars," Lucy said. "That was all. Fifty dollars . . ."

And it caught me then, what we were looking at. I had been too much on little Delie and Tyler, couldn't see past my darlings.

Lives. These were lives. All the people we knew and didn't know and Greerson, Waller, all the small evil men had been selling lives. Whole lives. My mammy, pappy, Delie, Billy— didn't matter. All bought and sold, people bought and sold for money, for work, to work to death. Heard once that when they worked the men down in the cane fields south, far south, they figured on the men being dead by twenty and seven. It was the way they worked it out. After they were twenty and seven they started to break and it was easier to just let them die and get newer ones, younger ones.

People. People bought and sold and each of them on these little pieces of paper, each of their lives down to a slip of auction paper. "Answers to name of . . ."

Swore then, swore in my mind so I suppose it's the same as swearing in the open and I hope God he don't get to keeping too close a track on those things. Swore at all the evil that men could do and I cried some with Lucy, cried for the people on the small papers we read in the yellow light from the lamp.

We stopped for a bit and sat, getting sad, but then I shook my head. Crying wouldn't help. "We have to eat something now. So we can keep going."

She took out one of the hams. We didn't have a knife but there was broken glass from the windows and I found a piece and sliced two chunks, thick with fat and smelling of hickory smoke. The smell must have been more than I thought because twice men came to the door while we were eating. One white and the other the same black man who had been beating Greerson. The white man he just looked in and moved on, scared looking, a white face flashing in the lamplight and gone. The black man he came in and we gave him some ham and he chewed it quiet, sitting in the corner, didn't talk to us, never a word and then he left, nodding his thanks for the ham while we went back to the papers.

More lives. We looked all night, paper on paper, and I stacked the ones we read in a neat pile. I couldn't bring myself to throw them away meaning what they meant and just at first gray dawn, sun just starting to help the lamp, Lucy she found it.

"Two children, one boy answers to name of Tyler, girl answers to name of Delie, to be auctioned together or separately—"

I snatched the paper away from her and read but it didn't say more. Just that, to be auctioned. My babies, to be sold. Together or separately? Not that, not apart, not all of us apart. Where were they, when were they sold, who bought them, who bought my babies, my life?

Nothing more on the paper. I turned it over and over but it didn't give nothing. Couldn't think, couldn't do, couldn't make my brain get working again.

"We have to keep looking," Lucy said. "There might be more paper on them." And she picked up another piece, then another, and I nodded and we kept going, kept looking and finally, eyes burning from smoke and no sleep and reading in the dim light all night Lucy she found it again.

"Two young Negro children, answer to Delie and Tyler, sold to William Chivington of New Orleans without auction for three hundred dollars."

I took the paper, hands shaking. Only thing else was the date. One day after they were taken from me. There was no auction. Greerson he must have been worried about what was coming. Wanted to get his money and run, only he didn't run far. Just to his yards. Low man, low as a snake's belly, he laid dead now in the yard where he caused so much misery.

But we had something now. We had a name, the name of the man who bought my children. We had a name and we had a place.

"Where," Lucy asked, "is New Orleans?"

"It's where we're going." Had hope now, had a name, a place. Had hope. Had *something*. "It's where we're going."

FIVE

"Easy say," Lucy said, "hard do, this going to New Orleans business."

She was right.

Was different then. No maps, no trains—least none that would carry us—no way to know how to go. We'd been on the plantation all our lives, all the lives before us, didn't know anything but the fields and the quarters and what we read in papers and books we stole.

Suddenly all that was changed. We're loose, we're moving, we're free, and I didn't have a tiny idea in my head where we were going, which direction, how far—nothing but a name. New Orleans.

Figured it had to be south. Man buying my children wasn't going to head north into the blue army. Had to go south.

I knew south. Place on your right when you face the rising sun, that's south. North is on the left, left side for freedom, south is the other. The bad way.

So I started walking. That night, right then, and Lucy she followed and we made less than a mile when I started in to weaving and Lucy said, "We've got to get some rest."

I knew she was right. We'd been up so long I was seeing things, hants and specters and such, glowing in the road ahead, and my body just quit.

"Over here," Lucy said. "There in the corner of that fence there's some slick willow. Here, lay down and rest." She took her extra shift out of her sack and I laid in it, smelling of ham. I closed my eyes and wanted to say thank you, wanted to tell her I had my own shift in my own bag and she didn't have to give me hers, but nothing came, no hants nor specters nor even dreams. Just sleep.

Somebody shaking me, pounding me around, and I had in my mind a picture of Greerson getting beat against the fence in the yard until my eyes snapped open. Gray light, small chill of morning air, not quite dawn.

"Come on!" It was Lucy. "There's going to be a battle. Come see."

I still had sleep in my brain or I wouldn't have gone. Didn't have time to be watching no battles with my children gone. But I was never one to think straight when I woke up so I followed Lucy up to a small rise a stone's throw away.

"I came up here this morning just before first light to take care of my doings and there they were fixing to fight. Looks like the whole army. . . ."

Wasn't the whole army. I read on things about the war later and learned that it would have been considered a small battle, compared to Gettysburg or Antietam.

But it looked big then. Below us was a shallow valley, went out about a mile and rose in trees on the other side. Trees just starting to show. Closer to us, less than half a mile, were two lines of men.

I wasn't good at counting then. Hadn't learned numbers except to slave count. Count to five, make a mark, count to five, make a mark, then count the marks. Way to count chickens or ducks or portions of corn flour. Counting that way, slave counting, I came to over a hundred men on each side.

The ones on the left were an even line, blue coats, almost clean. The other side the troops were ragged looking. Some had gray on, most just tatters of homespun or linsey and 'most half of them were barefoot but they stood in a straight line. Out front there were officers on horses and I wanted to go.

Wanted to leave but I couldn't. Like watching a storm coming. You knew it would come, knew you had to get in under something but you couldn't stop watching.

"What are they waiting for?" Lucy said and I looked and saw her eyes were shining like she was going to get food. Maybe more.

"You want this?"

She nodded. "They're all white, ain't they? I hope they all kill each other. Wouldn't bother me if every damn one of them died."

She said it soft, almost like she was praying, and there was a time, knowing only Waller, there was a time when I would have been with her but I shook my head. "They're all white but all whites ain't bad."

She stared at me. "Why, *listen* to you—have you gone feeble?"

I pointed. "Half of them are fighting to keep you in slavery but the other half are dressed in blue. Fighting to make you free. Fighting and dying and for you . . ."

They were done waiting.

The ragged side raised their rifles and fired. Some blue men fell. Then the blues fired and some of the ragged men fell. Then they all reloaded and fired as fast as they could. Sounded like a rattle, a giant rattle being

46

shaken or somebody tearing all the coarse cloth in the world. So loud you couldn't think.

Before it fairly started the smoke was so thick you couldn't see. Just red flashes and the tearing noise and then loud yelling, yips and yoops, and then some of the raggedy men could be seen running from the smoke, running away.

Then quiet except for screams. I thought it was from more fighting but a soft morning breeze came up and blew the smoke off and I could see the screams were from the wounded.

Laying all over the ground like broken toys, busted dolls, some crawling, pulling with their arms because their legs didn't work. Terrible damage. Only been three days of war and freedom and all I'd seen was terrible, terrible damage. Waller with the bayonet through him, bodies in the ditches by the road, Greerson dead, burned buildings and now this, butchered and torn men, men with parts coming out of them, dragging on the ground, dying, screaming.

Lucy her smile was gone and she must have been thinking like me because she said, "Freedom sure costs a heap, don't it?"

I thought we ought to go help. Either side it didn't matter. Men treated that way need help, some comfort, but two wagons came from around the hill said Ambulance on the side in big letters and started picking up wounded men from both sides.

"We'll go now, I 'spect," I said, and stood and started walking. Lucy she hung back a bit then caught up with me and her eyes were shining again only this time for different reasons. Crying, soft tears. She didn't say anything about it for over a mile, walking south, and then she just repeated herself.

"Freedom sure costs a heap." And she never talked on it again. I wondered how it could be that grown men could stand not forty paces apart and shoot each other down, just stand and shoot and reload and shoot until a bullet finds you. Seems nothing would be worth that.

We walked until the sun was overhead, heading south, and finally came on somebody who told us where to go. There'd been people moving on the road all along. Soldiers running this way or that, horses with officers galloping up and back and twenty or thirty black people. They weren't moving like the others, not aimed at going anywhere, just most of them away.

One man stopped us. Old man, shiny black with almost white hair and he waggled a finger at us. "It ain't going to last."

"What ain't going to last?" Lucy asked him.

"This freedom. The South will take it back soon as the war is over. They get done killing each other we going back to chains."

Wasn't true of course and I knew it then too, knew it would last. But not all the Northerners were friendly when they went by. There was some to call us bad names and would have kicked us hadn't we moved off the road and that made people worry that as soon as the fighting was done things would all go back the way they were.

"Where is New Orleans?" I asked the old black man.

"New Orleans? Child, why do you want to know that?"

I told him about my children. "I'm going to get them back."

He nodded. "I hope you do. I hope you do. I don't know where it's at, New Orleans. I think it's south and west about the same amount and it must be a far piece because my master went there once and was gone near half a year getting there and back. I recollect he said it was south and west about the same amount. Is that ham I smell in the sack?"

Had to give him a piece. I wasn't against sharing but most we met were hungry and did they see it the ham would go faster than grease on a griddle. He chewed slowly because he didn't have any teeth, only gums, and I took the time to ask him, "What is New Orleans?"

I didn't know much but one thing I did know—no excuse for not knowing when you could ask a question.

"Why, child, it's a city. A big city. My master he told us it was so big you couldn't see it all in a day. A big, big city . . ."

We set to walking again and an officer on a horse came along presently and stopped us and asked after the Glenrose plantation. I remembered the name on a burned gate.

"It's about three miles back," I said. "Would you know how to get to New Orleans?"

"New Orleans? You don't want to go there—it's still in rebel hands. Not all of the South is free yet."

"I've got children sold there . . ."

"Ahh. I see. God, this whole thing is . . . an abomination. Well, as the crow flies, which is I imagine the direction you'll walk, it's about three hundred and fifty miles almost due southwest."

I thought on it and couldn't make the number work in my mind. "How far is that—three hundred and fifty miles?"

He looked at my legs. "You can probably walk, at a steady pace, thirty-five miles a day. That means it will take you about ten days to walk to New Orleans—if the weather holds fair for you."

There, I thought. That's a good number. Five and a mark and five more and we're there. I walk faster I could get there quicker. "I thank you."

"Don't hurry. There's going to be a big fight down there and we'll win. You wait until after the fight and you won't have to worry about bounty hunters taking you back for the reward."

Knew about bounty men. Any slave that runs off can be caught by any man and turned in for a reward of hard money. I never had any hard money except a penny I found once but I knew money was a powerful drag on people.

We walked all that day, moving off the road for soldiers—Lord, I couldn't believe how many blue-coated soldiers there were. How could the grays ever even think on winning?

Men carrying rifles were all on foot. Sometimes big guns went by on wheels pulled in back of boxes on wheels by horses. Men sitting on the boxes. I 'spected it was the wheeled guns that made the thunder though I hadn't seen one fired yet and I thought if rifles carried by men could do such a terrible damage what could the big guns do?

Rip the sky, I thought. Rip men from their

souls, tear the sun open, kill like a bad wind. Scared me watching them go past even wearing blue coats. Big guns, hard men, faces dirty with smoke and death.

And more. I was having trouble with Lucy. Or starting to have trouble.

There was some to say I had a prettiness about me. Delie she had a broken piece of looking glass and I studied on it for some time but couldn't see it. I was too tall, too strong looking to be comely.

But Lucy she was different. She had the colty look that comes on young women. Spry legs that the slave-shift barely kept from prying eyes and she smiled at everybody and I thought, somebody don't marry her soon she's going to bust.

Something about her look, the way she moved, her smile made all the men look at her. Was like I wasn't even there. Look past me, over me, around me to see Lucy. Men almost fell off the wheeled boxes with the big guns looking back at her and sometimes the walking soldiers would trip and fall on the man in front to watch her.

By afternoon I knew something had to be done so I took Lucy off the road into some whistle willow and sat her down. "Give me that extra shift."

She handed me the shift from her bag. "What are you doing?"

"Covering temptation," I said. "Before it turns to something worse."

I took my sewing bag out, ripped cloth from her second shift and sewed a top on the one she was wearing to cover what men shouldn't see, then sewed some more on the bottom to hide those legs.

"I look like a feed sack," she said when it was done. "Like a bag of potatoes."

"Good. Now let's get to walking." I handed her some of my corn bread. "Chaw on this and stop smiling."

"Stop smiling?"

"At the men we meet on the road. Stop smiling and look down and don't take on such a wiggle when you walk past them."

"Well, I declare!" She stopped and stamped her feet in the dirt. "Is there a thing I'm doing *right?*"

I had to laugh.

"And I *don't* wiggle. It's just the way I naturally move . . ."

I started off walking again and set a good pace and she caught up soon, the mad gone, the smile back. You couldn't stop that smile with a hit from a shovel. But the dress helped and she did look down when we met soldiers

and there wasn't near the tripping and falling
going on.

We walked until the sun was high and would
have walked more 'cept we had to find water
to drink and that brought us on to the work of
scavengers.

SIX

Thirst come on us hard when it got warm, then hot, and there wasn't a brook or spring to find. Not that it would have helped since there seemed to be dead horses in every opening. Never saw anything so hard on horses as war. In the fields where they'd had battles the dead horses were so close you could walk on them without hitting ground—'most as bad as the dead men.

"We'll have to find a well," I said. "Pull into a plantation and find water. Maybe a jar to carry some in. I should have thought when we left."

"You were hurryin'," Lucy said. "You were in a powerful hurry."

We came on a gate with the name of Sunacres on it and started down a long lane with tall elms on either side. Would have been pretty hadn't I known that slaves planted every tree, made every rock fence and rail corner, hand-shoveled the lane.

Something wrong. I could feel it before we came to the house—white and big and ugly with four white posts holding the front roof up. Little smoke here and there, no black people, no white people showing. Dead dog in the yard, dead long enough to have clouds of flies on it, dead horse by a paddock off to the side. No chickens. Nothing.

"I don't like this," Lucy said, whispering. "Let's get water and get out of here. . . ."

There was a well with a hand pump in front of the paddock by the dead horse and I wanted to go there and get a drink but something, some call, kept pulling me towards the house. Just to see it, I thought, to see in a big house. Maybe nobody there. Just a peek. Stupid.

"Sarny, have you lost your brain?" Lucy saw me walking to the house. "Get *back* here!"

But I was going to see it. Up the steps, watching, listening. Didn't hear nothing. Inside to a tall room with stairs going up the back and I couldn't help but hold my breath.

Some bad things were done there. Everything torn apart and busted, blood on the floor. Bad things. Terrible things. But still the richness was there and I thought nobody, not a soul, should live like this, should have this, especially when it came on the backs of others. Pretty colors and gold seemed to be on every corner, every decoration.

"Lucy," I said, "come see. Come see how they lived here."

She came in but stopped just inside the door and made the hex sign. "There's bad here—see the blood? Bad."

That's when I heard it. Small sound. Like a puppy would make. Little noise, whimper.

"It came from upstairs." Lucy heard it too. "It's witches' sounds. Let's leave . . ."

But it wasn't witches. Too soft for that and besides, I never heard a witch's sound. Never saw a witch. Didn't believe in them. You could believe the Bible or you could believe witches. I believed the Bible.

I moved to the stairs at the back of the big room and walked up them slow, thinking that women came down this in fine gowns. Walked down pretty and soft in fine gowns.

Sewed by slaves. Couldn't stop the thinking. Everything pretty here was done by slaves.

At the top of the stairs was a dead man. White, old enough to be bald, blood on his shirt, and it stopped me. His eyes were open and staring at me 'cept not at me but past me and I remembered old Delie saying when somebody died the last thing they saw stayed on their eyes.

Somebody killed him. Was that still there? The sight of that? I called God to help me, make my heart stop pounding so hard, make my breath come even.

There. More sound, small crying. Not a dog. Maybe a woman, or a child.

"You're touched," Lucy whispered, and I jumped. Hadn't heard her follow me. "This is bad, all bad."

But I couldn't stop now. Moved down the hallway past the man's body and found the body of an old woman. White too, of an age to be married to the man. Eyes closed and blood on her front though not as much as the man.

Past her the body of a young woman, white, 'bout as old as Lucy and I won't say more on her because it was worse than dead. Worse than all the dead in the field after the battle. Worse.

Still there came the sound and I went into a bedroom 'most as big as many people's houses, bigger than the slave quarters at Waller's. Everything was torn apart, tables and chairs turned, pictures pulled off the walls, but even with that there was a feeling of richness. Blankets off the bed would make a pretty dress, curtains would make a gown. Small rooms off to the side of the bedroom held clothes and I didn't know they were closets. Didn't know what a closet was then.

The sound came from the closet and I looked back in where it was dark and saw a small shape in the corner.

"Come out of there," I said. "We ain't going to hurt you."

Little white boy. Younger than my Tyler. Couldn't have been much over his second year. He didn't come out so I reached in and fetched him out by the arm.

"What's your name?"

But he didn't answer. Just kept whimpering like a puppy and I looked up to the Lord and wasn't all that happy with Him for treating me like this. "Now what am I going to do?"

Lucy she thought I was talking to her. "Do? Why, we're going to leave this house and go to New Orleans, that's what we're going to do."

"And the boy?" I held him close, thinking on Tyler. "What about him?"

Lucy she looked at me like I was crazy. "You're going to leave him and get out of here. Are you thinking on taking him and raising him?"

"Don't see a bunch of choices 'cept take him."

"How far do you think we'll get carrying a white child?"

I shook my head. "I don't know. But he's needing help and it don't much matter what color he is, does it? Might be we could take him to a white family along the way. Just take him down the road a bit—"

"Just a bit? How many families you seen so far that would take in a strange boy?"

She was right. We hadn't seen anybody in shape to take in boarders. We hadn't seen anybody at all except people moving on the road and soldiers and bodies.

"We still can't leave him. He's too young to live on his own and there ain't anybody else. . . ."

And that is how we came to have Tyler Two.

SEVEN

"Something's broke with the part that lets him talk."

Lucy she was sitting with Tyler Two in the light from the fire. We had stopped for the night and I didn't much want to have a fire but it seemed even worse without the light so we moved back into a thicket so the light wouldn't get out and made the fire small.

We were coming on to being rich. Before we left the plantation Lucy she found a wheelbarrow with an iron wheel and high sides and we took some blankets and matches and cornmeal and a jar of grease from the kitchen plus three jars to haul water. I found some rolls of heavy thread and string and a packet of needles that I put in my sewing kit. Lucy she found a big butcher knife and two spoons. I felt some bad taking all of it thinking it was stealing in some way but the people there they weren't going to need it and we did.

We walked all day making good time with Tyler Two sitting on top of the load on the wheelbarrow. We must have passed enough people to make a town, blue-coated soldiers and free black men and women and sometimes white women and old people all moving along the road, and not one person said anything about two black women carrying a little white boy with corn-silk hair and sky-blue eyes on a wheelbarrow.

Folks they smelled the food in the wheelbarrow and wanted some but we had to stop sharing. There were so many people we would have been out of food in a short day.

You could tell the ones who wanted food. Black or white they were gant and walked weak and I wished we had a wagon full of corn bread and grease for them. 'Specially the children. There were many walking the road, some with older folks, some alone, and they all looked hungry and I couldn't see them without thinking on Tyler and little Delie but we just didn't have enough. Everybody headed north except us and the blue soldiers. We were going south. Some stopped to talk and they thought us touched for heading the wrong way.

"There ain't nothing but trouble, south," one old woman told us. "Promised land is north . . ."

Dark caught us still moving hard. It was Lucy's turn on the wheelbarrow and she finally just quit pushing. "We're going to stop now and make a fire and cook some cornmeal and pork fat and be like regular folks."

"Regular folks?"

"Yes, missy. I'm taking a rest. We can't just walk all night."

'Course she was right but I couldn't help myself. Kept thinking of how we found Tyler Two crying back in a closet, and of my own Tyler and little Delie. Stopping was the hardest thing for me to do but she was right.

Now we had some vittles in us and she was laying up next to the small fire and she was talking about Tyler Two.

"Must have been what he saw that keeps him from talking," she said. "The way his kin were treated. That poor girl—"

"Hush on that. Because he can't talk don't mean he can't hear. Just hush on all that and put it out of your head and get some sleep. We'll be moving before light."

I wrapped little Tyler Two next to me in a blanket. Small body next to me breathing, felt his chest rise and fall when he fell asleep and took some peace from it, but tired as I was I didn't go to sleep for a spell.

Thought of all we'd seen and done. How

fast it was all happening. One day I'm on a plantation and a man owns me. Can sell my children, sell me, whip me to death and nobody can say a word to him. Then a boy in blue comes along and sticks a bayonet through him and I'm free and I'm on my way to New Orleans with a wheelbarrow full of food and blankets and a white boy who can't talk.

Crazy life.

Thought on Nightjohn. Just as my thinking closed down for the night I thought on Nightjohn and how he really started it all. Saved me. Hadn't we been able to read we wouldn't have found the paper about New Orleans that I kept in a pouch tied under my shift.

Nightjohn he gave me that. Gave me reading so I could find my children. Wondered about him. Was he still alive? He'd be some older now. Been five and another five and one year. Hoped he was out there still, making them to read.

Missed him. Missed Martin too, and little Delie and Tyler. But missed Nightjohn more in some way. I wanted to thank him and couldn't and that made me to miss him heavier.

Then sleep.

* * *

Things change.

First I had Delie and she was my mother. Not my real one but the only one I got to know. Then along came Martin and he was my family and then little Delie and Tyler and now all of them were gone.

Now I had Lucy. Cross between a daughter and younger sister. And Tyler Two and the wheelbarrow. New family.

Pushing the wheelbarrow when it was my turn gave me time to think. The wheel rolled on the side of the road like it was meant for it and it had a spoke sticking through the steel a little so every time it went around it made a small bump.

Pretty soon it was like music. When Lucy she pushed she started singing, using the bump for a beat, and when I was pushing it made me think.

I didn't count miles. Didn't know how to count three hundred and fifty and as long as it took us to do one or two I would have felt sick waiting for New Orleans.

Days were easier. We'd been traveling two since the officer told us ten and that left five and a mark and then three more. Eight days and we'd be in New Orleans.

Bump of the wheel was like a clock to me. Bump, tick, bump, tock, bump, tick . . . Working on another day.

But things change and by midday the clouds came up and it started in to raining. Soft at first and I hoped it would blow over but then it came hard and before long the road was too muddy for the wheelbarrow and we stopped under an old oak and made a shelter with the blankets. Didn't stop the rain but the oak took some of it and the blankets let some of it slide off so we didn't get as wet as we might.

It kept on raining through the day and we made a cold camp because we couldn't find any dry wood to light—though I did think to put the matches in an empty water jar so's they wouldn't get wet.

Rained all day into dark. The road was a mess and close as we were to it we got to watch the soldiers working at getting south. The mud churned under their feet like runny brown butter and soon they were in it up to their knees, mud sucking their shoes off. Some tried to walk out to the side but it soon was the same and then they just walked in it. The horses sunk to their bellies and the wagons and big cannons went down to their axles and it was near impossible for them to move but they kept going. Men screaming curse words and whipping the horses.

"War don't care," Lucy said, sitting under the oak with the blanket over us. "Don't care about people, don't care about horses, don't care about weather—war it just goes on no matter.''

I thought on a picture I'd seen in the big house where we found Tyler Two. Big old thing on a high wall with a fireplace. Showed some battle somewhere with men using big knives and spears, wearing armor. Everybody in the painting was stopped forever the way the painter he caught them. Knife in air, never come down, man screaming forever with spear through him.

It was the same watching the soldiers going by. Men pulling on wagon spokes, screaming at each other, calling God bad names, mud and pouring rain and fallen horses and mules all frozen some way. Pictures in my brain that didn't seem to move. After dark it kept raining and there was some lightning and I was worried it might strike the oak but it never did, never did, and with each flash I would see pictures like the picture over the fireplace. Men beating horses, screaming at each other except the sound wouldn't cover the thunder—flash of light and then gone.

Lucy she was right. War don't care. Don't care spit for nothing.

EIGHT

Rain didn't stop for two days.

It let up some the second day and I thought it might clear but then it came on again and just kept coming.

The soldiers had a kind of slick cloth to keep the rain off their backs, hung around them like a tent, and Lucy she found three cloths soldiers had cast off or lost.

The blankets were soaked through and hardly slowed the rain down so we tied the three slick sheets together with bits of string and made a shelter that only leaked a little at the seams. Made some difference but camp was still cold. We ate cold ham—getting down to the end of it—and I saved the last of the corn bread for Tyler Two. Young bellies need that break-down food.

He still didn't talk but I saw him smile once when a soldier slipped and fell in the mud. I thought on it. Young are tough. Come back quick long as they aren't reminded of what brought them down.

Took me to distraction, sitting waiting for the rain to stop. Had a dream that little Delie and Tyler were on a train. Never seen a train 'cept for a drawing in one of the newspapers we stole back at Waller's. Big thing, ran on some kind of rail and they said it went fast. In the dream I thought here I sit in the rain while little Delie and Tyler are on the train going away from me. Made me want to run, catch up, and I woke with my legs moving like I was running.

Middle of the third night I was asleep and suddenly woke up. Still, quiet 'cept for men and horses moving on the road, and for a speck I couldn't think on the difference. Then I realized it had stopped raining.

Cool breeze and stars all over the sky.

"Wake up." I shook Lucy. "Wake *up*."

She shook her head free of sleep. "What's the matter?"

"The rain stopped."

"It's still dark."

"I don't care. Same as war for me. War don't care, I don't care. Sarny don't care if it's dark anymore. We're going."

Stupid. But I just couldn't sit any longer. Mud was still some bad and the wheelbarrow proved evil in the dark. Found every rut there was. But we started and I wouldn't stop and by light we had made a good two miles, maybe more. The morning sun baked the mud dry in no time and then it was just a job to dodge ruts which took no work when we could see.

By dark we were in different country. More hills and not so many plantations. Some swamps between the hills, and water now and again—ponds and such. I had never fished but Delie she told me about it and I thought there might be fish in some of the ponds and wished I had some line and hook since we were running low on meat.

We made corn bread that night when we stopped, and had it with ham. Tyler Two he wanted more but I didn't see where more food was coming so I made everybody eat short. Figured we still had seven or eight days to New Orleans and didn't know what would happen when we got there. Maybe there wasn't food there either.

Didn't matter because the next day we were in a battle and the day after that we met Miss Laura and everything changed again.

No warning when it came.

It was just before soft evening. Sun still high and hot and the mud turned to dust. Soldiers moving along in the heat too tired to swear, horses wet with sweat, and it was Lucy's turn on the wheelbarrow when I looked up on a ridge maybe five stone throws away and there's a line of raggedy men. One second they weren't there, then they were, spread across wider than two hands held out.

For a blink nobody else saw them. All the men in dust and some looking down and then the men on the hill raised their rifles and I heard somebody swear and yell, "Rebs!"

And they shot.

Like bees all around us. Bullets whistling by like bees, little hissing sound. We would have been hit sure 'cept a team of horses stood between us and the men on the hill. I heard the bullets hitting the horses and they grunted and went down and I grabbed Lucy and Tyler Two and pulled them back off the road and down into a small ditch no higher than a rabbit.

Everything went to pieces. The men on the hill reloaded and fired again and again and men fell around us, some dead and some about to be dead and some screaming and more horses were hit and they screamed 'most as bad as the wounded men. Bullets were as thick as flies and you could hear them hitting things over and over. Horses, men. Dead men were hit just laying on the road and I was sure we'd die.

Even if we weren't shot flat out those on the hill were gray fighters and we were with the blue. Did they come on down and find us I didn't think they would be gentle.

But the blues weren't about to let that happen. Took them some minutes but pretty soon they had pulled two of the big guns around and loaded and fired up at the ragged line. I never heard such a sound—so loud it seemed to come from inside my head. God sound. Big wagon guns blew so hard when they fired they were flung back on their wheels and the men would roll them up and load them and fire again and again until the men on the hill couldn't stand it and ran below the top of the hill line and were gone.

Terrible then. Horrible. Horses shot to pieces but still alive kicking and trying to get up until men came around and shot them and wounded men pulling themselves off the road into the ditch.

"God," Lucy said. We were still laying down not sure it was done and she said it over and over again, holding her hands over her ears. "God, God, God . . ." I thought at first she was swearing but she wasn't. Was praying and I prayed myself, holding little Tyler Two under me and praying.

Didn't see no ambulances coming and knew now we had to help. Nobody else did.

Soldiers who weren't wounded just walked away from those who were. Cut dead horses out of harness, doubled up wagon guns on horses that could still pull and off they went.

"Help them," I told Lucy. "Help them that's been hit."

"What do I do?"

I stared at her. "Why, you ease them, just ease them. Give them a smile and try to find a rag to bandage the wound . . ."

Easy say hard do, as Lucy liked to say. For bandages we didn't have anything but our blankets and the shirts off the men who were wounded. Some of them hit two, three times there wasn't much to bandage, wasn't much to do but sit and hold their hand while they slipped away.

Just boys. One man with stripes on his sleeve, older man, past his prime, died looking at his feet. But mostly just boys and they died hard, asking for their mammies or sweethearts and wanting us to tell them it would be all right.

It wasn't. Some not wounded so bad, hit in the arm or cut fine by bullets passing close, they got up and started walking back north. We eased the rest the best we could and just at dark some men they come in ambulances and started loading.

Before they'd pick the soldiers up they'd rip

their shirts open to show their bellies. Seemed stupid so I asked one when Lucy and me were helping to load them.

"We look to see if they've been hit in the guts. If they've been hit there we can't help them. Gut wounds might live a day or two but they always die so we just leave them."

Said it like he was talking about meat. Said it while we're stepping past men with belly wounds just laying there. Heard every word he said and knew they were going to die. Lucy she turned away and I could see she was crying and I felt stinging in my eyes.

The ambulances left and there were still four men there on the ground, all hit in the bellies and though they cried and were the most pitiful thing I'd ever seen the ambulance drivers turned their teams and left without them.

"We'll stay." Lucy she said it like there wouldn't be any arguing and I nodded.

"Yes. We'll stay awhile."

Didn't take two days. We couldn't move the four men and they were scattered some apart so we'd sit with one and then another and hold their hands. They were all thirsty and I tried giving water to one but he screamed when it went to his belly and so we stopped.

We cried some more. They cried. One gave

me a letter soaked with blood that he had inside his shirt and asked me to send it to a girl name of Margaret and I did too. Carried that letter over a year and then sent it.

One long day. Longest day of my whole life except one. The last one he passed over the next evening, almost exactly one day after the battle. Soldiers they kept marching past, heading south, but when they saw us they didn't help. Turned their eyes away and walked by fast and Lucy she said, "They don't want to see what can come on them later."

I think she was right. I thought on burying the dead men but all we had to dig with was the butcher knife and I thought they'd come and get the bodies later anyway. I prayed over them as much as I could remember from prayers Delie and I said. Since I didn't have anything to use for writing I remembered on their names. Not last names, just first. One boy he looked at me a long time and said, "My name is Carl. Please don't forget me."

I started crying thinking on it. Crying now writing on it. They were all going to die and nobody would know where they died or even who they were so I got their names and remembered on them.

Elijah.

Robert.

Jim.

Carl.

I see them now the way they were then. Young, scared and dying and I remembered on them.

Still do.

NINE

Later I was never sure whether Laura she found us or we found her. Didn't matter so long as we found each other, way I look at it.

When the four boys died we left that place and kept on moving south. There were more and more soldiers and guns and wagons moving on the road, so many of them that it made traveling hard and slow because we had to get off the road so much to let them go on by.

Slowed us down to a frog crawl. By this time we were running short on food and when we went by a plantation name of Haven Hall we turned in. Figured to see if they had some vittles and halfway down the lane coming to the house there stood a field of sweet corn to the side.

'Course the soldiers had been at the corn and most of it was gone. But corn it don't all come ripe at once and the ears too green for the soldiers had come ripe for us.

We picked enough for a feast and set to eating them raw. Tyler Two mostly gummed but he got some down and Lucy nodded. "Maybe we make a fire and roast a few ears he'll get more into his belly. Raw corn is hard to pull loose."

"I'd like some roasted ears myself."

So we found some wood and made a small fire at the side of the cornfield and when it burned down I pushed some ears we hadn't shucked into the coals. "Won't take but a mite."

And looked up to see a carriage coming down the lane from the plantation.

Ain't much on knowing carriages. Waller had one he thought was fancy and I 'spect it was pretty—shiny black with leather seats oiled, harness shining in the sun—but it wouldn't hold a candle to this one.

Closed in with soft red curtains over the windows and a small door on each side. Muddy here and there but still shiny with big wheels and a team of matched gray horses. Big black man driving the horses, sitting up on top with the reins coming back tight, like he was holding the horses from running. Wearing a black suit and a small round hat with a feather sticking up from it near a foot. He pulled the team up next to our fire and they fidgeted, stamping to go. Little spit from their lips where the bit went through.

Lucy's mouth dropped open and so did mine. Whole thing didn't belong. Not anymore. It was from before, fancy carriage being driven by a black man.

One of the curtains slid open and a woman's face appeared. Prettiest white woman I ever saw. Oval face, black hair pulled back with a silk scarf over it, brown eyes as big as a plate and white teeth. I could see Lucy stiffen and knew she wasn't going to take any sass off this woman and neither was I. Days for that were gone too.

"Excuse me for interrupting your meal but I wondered if you girls might be looking for employment."

Soft voice. Like honey over warm milk. Almost dripped with soft. Didn't know what employment meant but I didn't want to sound dumb. Didn't matter. Lucy jumped in.

She looked up at the driver. "You don't have to be working for her like this—slavery is done. Those blue soldiers are killing it. You can get down off that buggy anytime you want."

He smiled and shook his head. "I'm not a slave. Not now. I work for Miss Laura for money."

"I do not believe in slavery." The woman she pushed the curtain open wider. "I am offering you both a job helping me travel. I can pay each of you twenty dollars a month for the time I need you, and if you are suitable, the employment may continue after I reach my destination.''

She talked so fine. Words just floated out of her, lighter than air, all big and said just so. I couldn't help smiling thinking on it. Was like music. And twenty dollars a month. More money than I ever knew there was, just for a month's work. Real pay for work, pay in money. Used to dream about it. Working for money to earn enough to buy my freedom. Some did it on other plantations but Waller he would never have allowed it. But I shook my head. "I can't. I've got to find my children in New Orleans.''

She smiled again. "But my dear, that's perfect. I'm going to New Orleans.''

And that's how we came to be with Miss Laura.

There's some to say later that Miss Laura wasn't a moral person but most of those people have trouble with their own morals. Miss Laura she became a good friend to me, almost a mother like Delie, and without her I maybe wouldn't have had a life at all so I don't think too much on her morals. Just think on her as a friend.

'Course then I didn't know what I know

now. She opened the door of the carriage and motioned to the boy. "He can ride inside with me with one of you. I'm worried that he may fall off. The other one can ride on top of the carriage with Bartlett. I'd let you both ride inside but there isn't any room. I . . . liberated . . . some food from Haven Hall."

I saw inside the door she was holding open and she was telling the truth. The whole inside was packed with sacks and jars. Must have been enough food for an army.

"I'll ride on top," Lucy said, and I nodded because I could see it coming. Bartlett he wasn't ugly and Lucy she couldn't help herself.

Tyler Two and me we climbed up into the carriage and after moving some bags and boxes around we made a small place to sit. I sat and Tyler Two he sat in my lap.

"I am Laura," she said. "Laura Harris. And your name?"

"Sarny." Started to say more but stopped. Didn't have a second name. "Just Sarny."

She nodded. "A sign of the times, dear. A sign of the times. And the little boy?"

"We found him. He don't talk. Call him Tyler Two."

"Tyler too?"

"Like the number. My own son is Tyler and my daughter is little Delie so I just called this little man after my own Tyler. Except he's Tyler number twò.''

"I see. And where are your own children?"

And so I told her all about Waller and little Delie and Tyler and selling them and how we found where they were going and all of it. All of it. And when I came to where they took little Delie and Tyler in the wagons she said a word I only ever heard men say and turned away and looked out the window 'cept the curtain was still drawn.

Told her all of it even the name of the man took my children and all the time I was sitting there talking I thought on how it couldn't be happening. Never talked to a white woman except to say Yes ma'am and No ma'am, and here I was sitting in a fine carriage with this beautiful white woman that talked like molasses telling her everything. Everything. And she nodded and smiled and cried, a touch of a white hankie to the corner of her eye, and all the time I thought this ain't so, this can't be happening.

But it was. All of it.

Carriage rode like soft cloth over water, compared to the wheelbarrow. I never thought I'd see on anything like it and even later when the world was new and I rode in buses and trains smooth as glass I still remembered on that carriage.

When I'd finished Miss Laura she looked in my eyes and reached across the seats and touched my hand, like the feather falling off a bird, and smiled and said, "I will help you find your children when we get to New Orleans."

"But how will you know where to look? I heard New Orleans is so big you can't walk across it in a day."

"I know the man who has them. Chivington."

"You know him?"

She smiled softly. "I know many men. It is my business to know men."

Oh Lord, I thought, I don't know what I did to set you to helping me this way but should you give me a sign I'll do it again and again. To hand me this woman who knows the man who has my children, who will help me. Thank you, Lord.

Didn't say more. Didn't want her to be not liking me. White or not, could she help me get back my children I'd do anything for her. Anything.

She opened the curtains and I leaned back in the carriage while little Tyler Two he went to sleep on my lap and I thought over and over again, thank you, Lord.

Thank you, Lord.

TEN

It was still slow. Better than the wheelbarrow, better as day is better than night, but still slow because the road it was jammed with soldiers and wheel guns and the carriage was too big to go around.

First thing on the road, we hadn't gone ten paces after we turned out of the lane into the traffic when an officer on a big bay, officer with all sorts of gold on his blue shoulder, he rode up alongside the carriage.

"What in blue blazes are you doing with this rig on this road?"

"Oh dear, I'm afraid I'm in the way." Miss Laura she smiled up at him through the window and I could see him start to melt. "I'm terribly sorry but I have an urgent need to get to New Orleans."

"New Orleans? But that's still in rebel hands."

"So I understand. Still, I have to get there. I'm sorry if this is disruptive but I have this letter of passage from Bret— I'm sorry, from General Carrington. Would this help?"

"Madam, General Carrington commands this whole sector. If he says you can pass, you can pass. Please allow me to furnish you with an escort to clear the way."

Learned from that. Men think they have power and some do but it's only show power. Like bulls getting ready to fight. All dust and pain. Women have the underneath power. Little push here, little push there and things happen. Men don't see it but it's so. They think they own everything can be done but it ain't that way. Watching Miss Laura I learned.

Things went some better after that. Still slow but faster than the wheelbarrow by three times and I settled back for the ride. Miss Laura she looked out the window some and looked at me some and looked at Tyler Two some and smiled now and again but didn't say too much.

The escort was four men on horses with a young officer kept coming back to the carriage to ask Miss Laura if everything was all right.

"Thank you for your concern," she'd say. "Yes, everything is fine." And she'd smile so sweet the man would go off all puffed up.

Once I smiled. Couldn't help it. He was just so puffy and full of himself. Little boy with a gun on a horse. She saw the smile and knew what I was looking at.

"Aren't men wonderful?" she said. "They can do so many useful things for us. All we have to do is let them."

"You really know the blue general?"

"Bret? Oh my yes. We're dear friends. I met him when he came to New Orleans before the war. I held a gala for him when he was promoted."

Saw it then. She turned her head to look out the window and the scarf over her hair pulled away and right there in back of her ear I saw it. Tight hair, tight little black curls. Frizzy hair. I stared. Couldn't help it. Last thing I expected to see against that white skin.

She turned back and saw where I was looking and smiled again but didn't say anything, just held her finger to her lips and shook her head a tiny bit and pulled the scarf down to cover it again.

I'd heard of them. Delie she told me about women who passed. Didn't say were they bad or good, just some were called octoroons and they passed. I thought, oh my, here she sits in all this riding a fine carriage with a letter from a general and a blue escort and inside she's as black as me.

Made me chuckle. Little laugh.

"What are you so happy on?" Lucy her face

suddenly came into the window, hanging upside down, big smile across it. "You look like you ate a whole pie."

"Thinking on life," I said. "Thinking on how life is upside down sometimes. Like you."

Lucy she swung back up and was gone and Miss Laura she waved her hand. "She seems happy."

"Lucy she's always happy. Especially with men. She's up there with Bartlett and that will keep her happy enough. Maybe keep Bartlett happy too."

"You needn't worry about Bartlett. He's a dear man and has been with me a long time. He's . . . not quite functional, if you know what I mean. He's a eunuch."

I didn't know what she meant. Lots of her words went around me then and maybe some still would. I'd get the main ones, almost all, but some of the important ones seemed to skitter past before I could get their meaning locked up to hold. Sometimes I'd ask but wasn't I careful I'd be asking *all* the time and I didn't want to look dumb. Don't think I am, never thought I was dumb, but a place in me didn't want to even look that way so I held back and didn't find out until later that she meant Bartlett had been cut when he was a small boy so he couldn't make children. Owner did it when Bartlett he was still a slave, before Miss Laura she bought him and gave him freedom. Hope there's a hell, I thought when I finally learned what it meant. Hope there's a hell and Waller is there and the man who cut Bartlett was there and Greerson was there.

Bartlett he turned out to be the finest, most gentle and understanding man I ever knew.

I hope there's a hell.

We were two days getting out of the area the general's letter of passage covered. That night we stopped in a plantation called Albemarle where the only person was an old white woman called us darkies and I thought I was going to have to tie Lucy down to keep her from killing somebody. Lucy she took to freedom right smart and wasn't anybody going to step on it.

Old woman she was gone in the brain and thought we were visitors from another plantation. Twittered around like an old bird. Soon as we got down from the carriage she came out on the front steps of the house. Everything run down and grown to weeds so I 'spect she'd been alone for a long time. The hedges hadn't been trimmed in more than a year.

"My lands, you should have written you were coming. We didn't expect you. Here, girl," she says to Lucy, "take the lady's wraps and bring us some cordials. Be quick about it."

"I ain't your girl and you ain't *about* to be giving me no orders!" Lucy she wasn't smiling but it didn't matter because the old lady she didn't want to hear her.

"Excuse me." Miss Laura she stepped down from the carriage, one small foot on the metal step below the door, other on the ground, floated down, Bartlett holding his hand for her to brace on. Didn't I know how much power she had I wouldn't have believed it was the same woman.

"We need to rest our horses and rub them down. Would you have a room or cottage for us to spend the night in?"

"Of course, my dear. Of course. I'll have the servants show your darkies where to put the horses."

And she turned and disappeared back into the house. Left us standing. No servants came—weren't any servants. Wasn't anybody but the old lady and soon as she turned she seemed to forget we were there.

"Well." Miss Laura she shook her head and put her hands on her hips. "I guess this means we'll take care of ourselves. So much for Southern courtesy." She looked around. Wasn't much to see. Couple of old sheds, hog barn, old quarters—nothing on *earth* could get me to sleep in there and I 'spect Lucy she felt the same—and a carriage house.

"There, Bartlett. Over the carriage house there seems to be a room. You unharness the horses and put them in the paddock in back of the shed. I don't suppose there is anything like grain on the place, but they'll be fine on green grass. We'll stay in the room over the carriage house. It probably leaks, but it doesn't look like rain."

Bartlett stood off to the side and had the team pull the carriage over near the carriage house, then went to unhooking them, and we went inside and up some steps to the room.

Dirty, dusty with old rat pellets everywhere but it looked dry. Way better than under an oak with rain dripping down your neck, I thought. Miss Laura she found a broom in a corner and handed it to Lucy. "Lucy, you sweep it down while we carry in some food and social comforts. Tyler Two can help you." She smiled. "And it's *not* an order."

Lucy she laughed and took the broom and soon there was a cloud of dust so thick you couldn't see through it.

We lugged and carried. Miss Laura she pulled as much as I did and when Bartlett he was done with the horses he helped us and before tight dark we had a couple of candles lighting the place and a blanket for each person on the floor. Almost seemed like a home.

"I don't see any lights at the house." Miss Laura she looked out a small window. "I suspect the old woman has gone to bed, which is all to the good. I didn't relish the thought of calling on her. She's a dragon."

She dug in a carpet bag Bartlett had brought up and came out with four plates, spoons and knives and forks, and had Lucy spread them on a blanket on the floor. "Now we're set. I'm sorry I don't have one for Tyler Two, but he's asleep anyway. Lucy, you did a splendid job cleaning—my compliments."

Lucy she smiled that light-up smile of hers and rearranged the plates like she'd been doing it all her life and hadn't been eating in quarters.

"Bartlett, I think this calls for a jar of preserves and some bread and cheese and a little ham, don't you?"

"Whatever you say, Miss Laura." He left and went down to the carriage and came back in a minute with a sack and we soon were eating cheese and ham and bread with apple preserves off of plates.

"No, no, Lucy, you hold the fork like this." Miss Laura she helped Lucy and I copied. Never used a fork before, only a spoon and the tip of a sticking knife. Never saw plates like these before. Held one up and you could almost see through them. Flowers painted all over them so pretty you could almost smell them. I was so hungry my jaw ached and I was chewing and started crying. Dumb. Seemed to be crying *all* the time. Couldn't help it. Miss Laura she saw it.

"Why, Sarny—what makes you cry?"

"Nothing . . ."

"Come now. Something is bothering you. What is it?"

"Just thinking on how it's always been like this for some people. All the time Delie and the rest of us were in the quarters having to live hard somebody was sitting eating with forks on plates with flowers on them. Just thinking on it made me sad for all of them before. That's all. Just thinking on it made me wet up. Don't mean anything much."

Miss Laura she leaned across the blanket and touched me on the arm. "We each live in our own time." Her voice was soft. Like she was talking to a little girl. Soft with love. "And we must do the best we can with our time. Those who came before weren't as lucky as us and we aren't as lucky as some who may come later. We must still live in our own time and do the best we can."

Lucy she was sitting still, listening, catching every word. Every word. And she raised up, put her fork down. "What do you mean *us?* You're talking like you're like we are—like you've had to live in a quarters."

"We all have our own quarters," Miss Laura said, voice still soft.

"Yes, but you're not colored."

Miss Laura she didn't say anything for a second but she looked at me, quick look, and then away. "Be that as it may, we all have our quarters."

She served us each a sweet preserved peach from a jar and we ate it with our forks, holding them the way she showed us, cutting small pieces and chewing them, tasting the sugar in them.

Bartlett he left to check the horses and came back in a minute. "They're fidgeting. I'm going to sleep in the paddock in case something comes to bother them."

He took his blanket and left and Miss Laura she stood up. "Well, let's get some sleep. I think we should be moving before daybreak, don't you?"

Lucy and me we just had our shifts, which we slept in. But Miss Laura she had to take off her dress and then one petticoat after another. Lord, I haven't ever *seen* so many petticoats. When she got down to a satin slip she spread a comforter on her blanket, took a pillow from a bag Bartlett had brought up and tucked herself in. Just before I blew the candles out I saw her reach in her handbag and take out a small pistol.

She saw me look at it. "One hates surprises," she said. "Especially when one is sleeping."

I blew out the light and laid there for a long time, not sleeping, thinking on all she had said and how we had to live and I thought, fine. I'll live in my own time. Long as I have my children to live with me.

Suits me fine.

ELEVEN

New Orleans it wasn't much. Like a lot of things the way we 'spected it to be didn't happen. I had in my mind towers rising to the sky. Don't know why. Nobody ever said it was that way but in my brain I had it pictured like that.

The war it ended three days after we spent the night at the old lady's. We were traveling down the road and suddenly the soldiers around us set to whooping and hollering. We had a new escort. Miss Laura she had another letter from another general. Lucy she said without thinking, "You must know 'bout every general there is."

"And many who aren't generals," Miss Laura said, smiling. "Yet."

The officer in charge of the escort stopped and talked to the soldiers who were hollering and then came back to the carriage.

"Great days," he said. "The war is over. They've signed a peace at Appomattox."

"Who won?" Miss Laura asked.

"Why, we did, of course." The officer smiled. "It was a foregone conclusion, wasn't it?"

"Of course." Miss Laura smiled up at him. "Of course it was—how could you be beaten? I was just joking."

And I thought she'd have said the same thing was she talking to a Southern officer and they had won but I didn't say anything. Woman knew how to live in her own time and make the best of it.

The travel went better after that and we made twice as much in a day and in two more days we came to New Orleans.

Wasn't so much. By the time we got to New Orleans we'd been through so many towns I couldn't remember their names. Big ones and little ones. Some of them Miss Laura she would keep the curtains closed on the carriage and sometimes we went through two towns in a day. Most of them were smoking and broken with people trying to pick up the pieces.

Finally we came around a bend in the road and Bartlett tapped on the side of the carriage top and said, "There's home."

Miss Laura she opened the curtains and pointed ahead. "There's New Orleans."

So I looked but didn't see much but another town on a good-sized river. River kind of curved around from the side and the town tucked in down to the edge and I was some excited but not by the town.

Thought on little Delie and Tyler. They were here. Turned to Miss Laura. "When can I get my children?"

She nodded. "Ahh yes. I had forgotten Mr. Chivington and your babies. Let me see—it's late afternoon now and will be evening before we get there. Chivington needs to be handled delicately—he's a fussy man, as I remember him."

"Doesn't he give me my children I'll kill him where he stands."

Miss Laura smiled. Small, tight. Nodded. "Yes. I understand. But it's possible that he doesn't have your children. He may have given them to somebody else or sold them or sent them off for one reason or another."

"He can't sell them. Slavery is against the law now. Done."

She sighed. "Yes. Slavery is illegal now. You're right, Sarny. But I'm afraid it isn't necessarily finished. There will always be slavery in some part of the world and always be men willing to buy and sell people."

Like a cold blade through my heart. All the fighting, the battles we saw to stop it and she says slavery will still be there. Sell my babies. No. He couldn't do that.

"Don't worry just yet. He hadn't had the children long, and the war just ended three days ago. It's simply that we must handle it carefully so we don't alarm him. If he feels threatened, he might never tell us where they are. We have to be nice." She stopped smiling. "At least at first . . ." She thought on it for a time, looking out the window. "I'll throw a welcome-home party for myself day after tomorrow and invite him along with others. It's short notice, but I think we can succeed. Once we get him relaxed and happy, we'll go to work on him. Can you wait two more days?"

"Have to." She was smart, smartest person I'd ever seen and trying to help me and I'd do anything she said but it cut bad, deep, having to wait.

Town was all noise, crowded with people, but there wasn't a sign of war. I found later there wasn't much fighting going on here. Bartlett he had to pull the carriage down to a slow walk and it took us near a half hour to work through the streets until he stopped the horses and Miss Laura she opened the carriage door and stepped down. "Home."

I climbed out holding Tyler Two and Lucy she jumped down from the top.

"Ain't this something?" she said, eyes wide, smiling at all the people walking past us. "Did you ever even *think* on a place like this?"

And I had to admit it was more than the other towns. It just kept moving. People all hurrying one way or the other. On one corner there was a man cranking a box that made tinny music and he had a tiny spit of dog on a string dancing on its back legs to the music.

Stupid, I thought. Dancing dog. What's it good for? But the man had a tin cup and people dropped pennies in it when they walked past. I wouldn't have done it. Pay a penny to see a dog dance. But some did and the man'd smile and crank harder.

All sorts of people. Black people, white people. Some in rags, both black and white, some dressed in fine clothes, both black and white, some pretty and some fence ugly, both black and white. For a breath I watched it, thought on it, marveled on it, and then I saw a small black head and thought on Tyler, almost called his name before I saw it couldn't be him. Too tall and I looked away, saw another black child and then another boy dancing to an old black man playing a fiddle for more people to drop money in a box on the ground.

Children everywhere and every one I looked at made me think on Tyler or little Delie and I had to hold myself to keep from running after them.

"Are you going to stand all day?" Lucy she

was back on top of the carriage holding a hat-box down to me. "We have work to do."

I shook my head. "Was thinking on Tyler and little Delie." I looked and was surprised to see Miss Laura she had gone. Big building with three floors, open place in the middle with black iron gate like bars, only made into pretty shapes. The gate was open and led into the open place full of green plants and vines that climbed the walls and a stairway up the side.

"Take some boxes. Bartlett and Miss Laura they went up those stairs on the side and down to a door. "Get to carrying."

I took an armload and headed up the steps, down a balcony to an open door and stepped in. For a bit I couldn't see much because of the boxes but Bartlett he was there and he took them from me and I looked around.

"Oh my . . ."

It was like a . . . a . . . I don't know what. I didn't know on castles then, hadn't learned on them, but that's what it was like. I was in a big room with high ceilings and paintings all over the walls and flowered wallpaper so real you could smell the flowers and tall windows with drapes made of cloth that caught the light coming in and seemed to glow inside. In the middle of the room was a large dark wood table, all polished and shined 'cept it had some dust on it. Over against the wall was a tall wooden box thing that I found later was a piano. It all took my breath away. "Oh my . . ."

Miss Laura she was standing there, holding Tyler Two by the hand to keep him in one place. "You like my little home?"

"You *live* here?"

She nodded.

"In *all* the rooms?" There were doors off to the side of the big room on both sides. Eight of them. Doors so tall I couldn't have reached the top standing on my toes.

She laughed. "Well, yes. Of course, you and Lucy will live in one, and Bartlett lives in one, and there is a kitchen in one, and two are for baths, and there are two other rooms for . . . other reasons."

"Bath?"

"A place to make water and clean up. I have two of them. One for you and Lucy and Bartlett and one for myself."

"You've got a place to do your doings?" I asked. *"Inside?"*

"Yes, dear. It's all the rage."

"Oh my *God*!" A scream from in back of me and I turned to see Lucy standing there holding a box, staring up at the room. Mouth open and eyes wide.

"Don't be swearing," I said.

"Didn't *you?*"

"It's just her house," I said, staying settled, but I couldn't help smiling. "And ours. We've got a bath. Inside." Was hard not to take on with it. I never in all my days thought anything like this was real and for me to be living in it— was hard to not take on with it. Inside bath. My Lord.

Miss Laura she went to one of the doors and opened it. "Here, see?"

Stuff in there didn't seem real. Big copper tub with handles at one end, some kind of seat with a hole in the top—I knew what it was for but didn't see how it worked, where it all went—and sink with a looking glass over it.

"What are the handles for?" Lucy asked. I wanted to but thought I'd already asked enough.

"Handles . . . oh, you mean the faucets. Those are for water. One for hot and one for cold. There's a large tank on the roof, and water is pumped up there for the apartments. In the basement there's a boiler that keeps it hot for the hot-water faucets."

"You mean you just turn that handle and you've got hot water?" I couldn't help myself. "That's all you do?"

"Try it. The one on the left."

I turned it. Wrong way of course, then the right way. Took a minute but then it was so hot it hurt my hand. Turned it off. "I never thought there could be such a thing. In the quarters we had to heat water in the big cookpot over the fire."

Miss Laura she held up her hand. "There are no more quarters. Ever. From now on you won't speak of them, and tonight you will both have a hot bath with French perfumed bubble soap."

She left the room and opened another door. "This will be where you three sleep— the two of you and Tyler Two, until we can find him a home."

We looked in the door. There was a bed and a table with a chair and another kind of half bed with a back on it—she called it a couch—and an oil lamp on the table with a milk-white chimney and there was a pointed thing in a stand on the table with some dark fluid in a little jar.

"What's that?" I asked. "With the sharp end."

"Why, it's a pen. There is paper in the drawer of the table. You can write letters if you wish, and Bartlett will send them for you."

I went to the table and pulled the drawer. Clean white sheets of paper. Pure clean. I pulled one out and put it on the middle part of the table. Took the pen and tried to make a mark but nothing came.

"You have to dip the point of the pen in the ink," Miss Laura said. "Just a bit on the end."

I dipped it. Black ink, black as me, and I wrote on the paper. Wrote BAG. In all big letters. Couldn't help it. Wrote BAG.

"What is that?" Miss Laura asked.

"It's the first word I ever wrote," I said. "First word I knew. BAG. Learned to read in a pit school."

Little sound and I turned and she was smiling at me, her eyes misting. She touched my arm and then she took me and hugged me and pretty soon Lucy she was there and the three of us were hugging and were my children there and Delie and Nightjohn and Martin I wouldn't ever have been happier.

Want to talk more on that bath. That whole first night in New Orleans.

We unpacked and Miss Laura she sent out for food—I never heard of such a thing. They brought shrimp and chicken and red beans and rice in metal buckets and we ate at the table off plates you could see light through and drank something Miss Laura called a cordial in crystal glasses that caught light from everywhere some way. Tyler Two he went to sleep on the bed in our room. I got to giggling after drinking the cordial—Lucy she got plain silly—and when we'd cleaned up the dishes in the kitchen where there was a sink and more hot water for washing, Miss Laura she said, "All right, who's first for the bath?"

I didn't want to be a hog for it so I held back but Lucy she didn't want to appear hoggish either and finally Miss Laura she took a straw from the broom and broke it in two pieces and held them out partly hidden in her hand.

"Short straw goes first."

I got the short straw and Miss Laura she took me in the bathroom, put a plug in the bottom of the tub and started water running. A little hot and a little cold but it still almost steamed.

"Take off your shift. You won't be wearing it again."

"What am I going to wear?" I pulled my shift over my head.

"I have uniform dresses for you and Lucy to wear, but tonight you're going to have a silk gown." She took a bottle off a shelf and sprinkled what looked like sugar in the water. Didn't smell like sugar. Smelled like flowers, like lilacs and red flowers that grow along the stream. Smelled so good I made spit. Made me hungry but didn't know for what. For summer, soft nights, soft talk, maybe Martin. The sugar made soapy bubbles that filled the tub.

"Get in."

I stepped into the tub, stood there.

"Sit down. Lie back and relax. Don't be nervous. Just relax. When you're done, those cloths on the rack are towels. Dry with one of them, put the gown on and sleep. I'll see you in the morning."

Miss Laura she left then, came back in a moment with two silk gowns, one for Lucy one for me, and left again without talking, closed the door soft in back of her.

I couldn't believe it. Was in it, smelled it, felt it and couldn't believe it anyway. Like being inside a warm flower. Smell all around, up, down, inside me in some way—soft lilac smell and hot water soaking. Laid there like a log. Water got deeper and deeper and I turned it off afraid it would run over and then just laid there, half floating, bubbles all up around me so I couldn't see much past my nose.

Closed my eyes and let everything slip away, just slip away from me, and didn't think on anything but the lilac smell until the water started to get cold and Lucy she couldn't stand it any longer and tapped on the door.

"Are you going to be in there all night?"

I dried with a towel and put the silk gown on. So soft it was like more bath. Dried my hair and let Lucy in. Showed her what to do, started her tub, poured in some sugar and told her about drying with the towel and the gown and went to my room.

Had in my mind writing something. White paper waiting, pen and ink right there. Had a thought on writing a letter to Delie telling her about things. Knowing she couldn't read it because she was dead didn't change it. Had it in my thinking to write to her anyway but I slid into the bed under the covers next to Tyler Two—Lucy she said she'd sleep on the half bed where Miss Laura she had laid some blankets—and there wasn't anything else I could do but sleep.

Soft hot water, soft smell of flowers still on me, soft silk of the gown next to my skin and soft feeling of the fine sheets on the bed and there wasn't anything for it but to sleep so I did and when I woke up it was a whole new world.

New Orleans

TWELVE

That first night Miss Laura she waited on us and that was fine. Fine. But she had hired us to do a job of work and when we got up the very next morning we had to get busy.

Miss Laura she seemed to know everything, know everybody, and she sat us down and told us our duties.

"Sarny, you will market and cook and help me socially. Lucy, you will clean and take care of the laundry and straighten the place up after any social event. As I said, you will be paid twenty dollars a month each plus room and board. Any questions?"

I didn't much know how to cook 'cept for quarters food—cornmeal, beans and pork fat, and I was pretty certain she wasn't talking about that kind of cooking. Didn't know what she meant by marketing and had no thought at all in my mind how I was to help her "socially." Started to keep quiet and knew it would do no good. "I don't understand how to cook, market or be social . . ."

She laughed. "Bartlett will show you at first. Don't worry, you'll pick it up fast. And Lucy, Bartlett will show you what to do as well."

"What do we wear?" It was still early and Lucy she had sleep in her eyes. "We can't do much in these gowns."

"You will wear uniforms. Bartlett will show you where they are."

After that any problem I had I just figured to ask Bartlett. He seemed to know everything.

"I'll need coffee and a light breakfast—one egg, two pieces of toast with strawberry jam." And she turned and went back into her room.

"Well," Lucy said. "I guess we get to work."

So we did and that first day it went about as bad as it could go. We put on our uniforms. Black dresses way better than the shifts. Bartlett he showed me how to make breakfast but it took me three tries to get an egg right and just figuring out the kitchen and the stove that burned some kind of gas would have been more than I could handle hadn't it been for Bartlett.

Strong and quiet. Never said a bad word or made fun of me. Would just smile and say, "No, Sarny, try that knob over there. Turn the gas down a mite. Don't boil the eggs quite so hard. Miss Laura likes them soft on the inside and just turning hard on the white.''

"I ain't ever going to get this . . ."

"Yes you will. Don't you worry. It'll all come easy to you. Just keep on keeping on and it will be fine.''

Then he'd go to help Lucy find a broom or mop and all the time Tyler Two he was hanging on Bartlett's leg. He hadn't started to talk yet but he was 'bout as wild as a pup, running back and forth, and he decided he belonged to Bartlett. Bartlett he was like a gentle bear. He'd pick the boy up and carry him with one hand while he showed us what to do, then set him down until Tyler Two he would run back and climb up his leg.

When I had the breakfast just right Bartlett he put it all on a silver tray and told me to take it in to Miss Laura.

I knocked on the door and went in and stopped again, mouth open, just like Lucy. Big room, high ceiling with a big bed in the middle. Bed had a roof on it. Four posts held the roof over the bed and soft cloth hanging down all around. Everything in gentle red so the room it looked almost hot. In one corner was a table like the one in our room and she was sitting there writing on small pieces of paper. She pushed the paper aside. "Put the tray down right here. I was just writing invitations for the party I told you about—the one we're going to invite Chivington to. Did you sleep well?"

I was so busy looking at the bed I didn't hear what she said. "I'm sorry—what did you say?"

"Did you sleep well?"

"Oh yes. Slept like a baby. I felt like I was sinking into the bed all night and Lucy she slept so hard I thought she died."

Soft laugh. "I'm glad you like it. I think I've needed someone like you for a long time."

Had me a question and I didn't want to ask it because it seemed too nosy but she saw it in my face. Woman knew everything. Saw everything.

"What's the matter?"

"Just wondering what happened before we came. Did you do all this your own self?"

"No, of course not. Bartlett did some, and I had another girl. Her name was Susie, and she worked for me for almost two years. She was very good, but somebody stole her."

"Stole her?"

She nodded. "It was still slavery times then. Susie was free, and I paid her the same as I'm paying you, but there were bounty hunters, and one day they took her when she was marketing. We never saw her again, never heard another word from her."

"Oh my . . ."

"Yes. It was very sad. I tried to find her but she had simply vanished."

"She might have been sold to the cane planters. They just worked people to death. We heard about them from Nightjohn."

"Nightjohn?"

"He was a friend. More than a friend. Made me to read." I told her the story, just a bit of it, how he came to know me.

"He sounds like a singular man."

Didn't know what it meant but liked the way it sounded. "Yes he was. Very singular." I left then so she could eat her egg before it got cold.

Bartlett he was there waiting for me holding Tyler Two like a package under one arm. Lucy she was busy cleaning and Bartlett he went to the front door.

"We'll do the marketing now. We need 'most everything there is to need. Lucky I had those eggs for the trip. There isn't even any salt."

I followed him outside and was surprised to find it was midmorning already. Sun was up, hot, little clouds here and there and such a bustle in the streets that it made me stare. I thought it had been full of busy people when we came the day before but it wasn't even close. People were jammed next to each other and everybody seemed to be yelling and pushing.

Bartlett he opened the gate and jumped in, dragging me by the hand, and we went along like chips in a river.

'Most everybody seemed to be selling something. The man with the dancing dog was still there. Man with no legs playing a fiddle on the other side of the street. No-count women, some black some white, all thick with paint were on balconies calling to men to come up, and weaving through the crowd were beggars and some men so drunk they could hardly walk. Middle of the morning and they were already drunk. In the road there were carriages jammed in with freight wagons all heading down to the river where I could see four big paddle-wheel boats that weren't there yesterday.

"Is it always like this?" I asked Bartlett.

"No." He shook his head and smiled back at me. "Sometimes it's worse. Don't worry, you'll get used to it."

Heard somebody yell a curse and then the crowd parted like water around a rock and two drunk men had knives and were going at each other, cutting and stabbing until one of them got the other one in the stomach and the wounded man walked away holding himself swearing. Crowd just closed up and kept moving.

There was so much happening I couldn't tell where we were going but before we'd gone too far we came to a strip of road where there were booths. Had canvas awnings out in front to keep the sun off and I never saw so much food in my life. Couldn't even *find* bacon grease and cornmeal or other quarters food. Was like there'd never been war.

Bartlett he jammed through the people and started in to buying. Bought rice and beans and a shoulder of pork and all sorts of different vegetables. Each time he'd ask how much it cost and no matter what the seller told him he'd shake his head and offer less. Then they'd go back and forth until they worked out a price and then he'd point to me and tell the seller, "This is Sarny. She'll be doing the buying from now on."

They'd nod and he would move on without picking up what he'd bought.

"Are we going to take it all on the way back?" I asked.

"Oh no. They'll deliver it right to the house. They all know who Miss Laura is. She pays once a month and never misses. They all love her. All right, now you try."

We were at a booth where they sold fish.

Didn't know anything about fish but I remembered the shrimp from the night before and pointed to a box of them. "I'll be wanting those."

"Oh you will, will you?"

Found myself looking on a man 'bout as big as Nightjohn had been. Carried himself straight up and down. Deep black with a wide smile and eyes that seemed on the edge of laughing. Found myself looking on my next husband. But I didn't know it then.

Then I just thought he was some city sharper figured he was going take a country girl first time she tried buying something. Wasn't about to let that happen.

"How much do you want?" he asked.

" 'Bout like this." I made a double heaping handful of them. "How much for this much?"

"Be 'bout thirty cents," he said.

Didn't even know much about money then but I shook my head. "That's twice too much and you know it."

"Twice? It ain't even enough."

"Bring it down or I'll move on to another booth. Must be somebody else selling shrimp around here. . . ."

"But if you go I won't see that fancy smile again."

"Shining me won't help. Bring the shrimp

down." But I could feel myself smiling and cheeks warming up just the same.

"I will if you'll tell me your name."

"Sarny. Now bring them down."

"I'm Stanley," he said. "And I want you to come back to my booth again when we can just talk some. Will you do that?"

"Not likely. You've probably got a bunch of girls come and talk to you."

"Not like you, Sarny. Not like you."

"I can't stand here and jaw all day long. You send those shrimp to Miss Laura's. Also send a couple of those fish over there."

"Catfish?"

I nodded. "And don't be trying to charge an arm and a leg for it. How much is it?"

"That would be twenty cents a fish."

"Too much."

"All right—fifteen cents."

Never ate on a catfish but had heard about them from other slaves and knew you fried them in a pan with bacon grease or lard. We moved on then before Stanley he could get to talking again.

"That was good," Bartlett said. "They always ask about twice as much as they figure to get, so you did good."

Tyler Two he started in to fussing and Bartlett he stopped at a booth where they had a jar of some kind of sticks with stripes on them. He got three of them and gave one to me.

Sweeter than honey. "What is it?"

"Hard candy. You like it?"

I nodded and kept it in my mouth and from that day on I had me a piece of hard candy every day. "Maybe we'd better get some sent back to Miss Laura's," I said. "You know, so Lucy she could taste it too."

He smiled and nodded and told the man in the booth to send back a parcel of them and we went on to finish marketing. So much new happening that my mind was taken up with it but I still couldn't forget Tyler and little Delie. The market was filled with children and every time I saw one about the right size I would start for him or her but of course it was never them.

Half a day we spent at that market. We must have bought enough food for a whole town.

"Who's going to eat it all?" I asked Bartlett as we started back for the house, still looking on every small body I saw, still hoping.

"Oh, don't worry on that. It won't last more than a week. Miss Laura she has guests 'most every night and they always want a dinner. Food don't last long."

Must eat like hounds, I thought. Must be some powerful hungry guests.

THIRTEEN

That man Chivington he brought my children right to me 'cept he didn't know he was doing it.

Miss Laura she had Bartlett deliver the invitations to all the people and the day of the party she took Lucy and me aside and sat us down and told us we had new duties for the party.

"Sarny, you will prepare all the hors d'oeu—"

"Prepare what?"

"Just ask Bartlett. Anyway, you will prepare them and put them on trays, and Lucy, you will serve them. Just go around and offer them to people. Bartlett will handle the drinks. When you've finished with preparing the food, Sarny, I want you to greet people at the door and take their coats. You can put them in on your bed but put them down neatly. After that you can help Lucy with the food and Bartlett with the drinks. Any questions?"

"How many people are coming?" Lucy she tugged at her dress to get it down. Everything she wore seemed to want to show her legs.

"I invited sixty but I doubt they'll all come. Then there's a four-piece orchestra for music, and some of the men may bring guests. I couldn't say for sure—perhaps forty."

Had to learn on numbers. They didn't mean anything but it didn't matter. We had our duties and I went running to Bartlett to learn how to make the fancy food.

Little things. Bit of cheese here, smoked fish there. Little corners of cut bread and some black fish eggs that tasted of salt so bad I couldn't eat them.

"They're called caviar," Bartlett said. "They come from Russia."

"What's a Russia?"

"It ain't a what, it's a place. A country far from here."

Had learned some on that. Knew that there were other places, that the world was round, all that from reading stolen papers. But I didn't know all the names or even very many and while I was thinking on it I went to Miss Laura. She was talking to Lucy about how to hold the tray.

"Excuse me, Miss Laura, but is there some other way to learn things so I don't always have to be coming to you and asking?"

"Why, of course, Sarny. You can read books. I have some in the study but not very many. But I will start getting them for you if you wish."

And that's how I started into learning. Figure reading is all right but you have to have something to read about and I didn't know so much I didn't even know what I didn't know. Just had to pick a place and start in to learning.

No time then. I worked on the food all day with Bartlett showing me now and then to get me started and by eight o'clock that evening when the guests were supposed to start coming I had me about twenty trays' worth and had gone a far way into the food that we had bought.

Had just a minute or two and I went into the bathroom and made sure I was clean—had a bit of flour on my cheek—and just left the room when the gong went off for the front door.

Was a tall man, thin, alone, 'bout the sickest-looking man I ever saw still alive, wearing dark clothes and had his hair all greased back.

"Am I too early?"

"No sir. Miss Laura she'll be just so glad to see you." 'Bout made myself sick I shined him on so much. But Miss Laura she said to make them all feel welcome and happy. I took his coat into our room and turned just in time for the gong to go again.

Then again and again and pretty soon they were coming so fast I couldn't keep up. Turns out Miss Laura she had invited all men and they had all come and many of them brought women with them. Not their wives, other women. Bell just kept dinging and I was running back and forth like grease on a griddle 'bout to go crazy and once I opened the door to a big man, heavy but not fat, and I looked up to take his hat and coat and Tyler and little Delie walked right past me into the room full of people.

Didn't see them at first because I was looking up and never, in all my days, did I expect it. Took the hat and coat and turned and they were standing there dressed in funny little suits that made them look silly. Tyler had a turban on.

"Tyler?" It was like a beef getting hit with a hammer. Just stood there. "Is that you?"

"Mammy? Are you my mammy?"

"Well, boy, what did you think?"

"Mammy!" Little Delie she knew right away. She threw herself at me, jumped up in my

arms and then I was down on my knees kissing and hugging both of them. Knocked that silly thing off Tyler's head and hugged them so hard their eyes bulged.

"Now see here." Man reached down. "What do you think you're doing with those children?"

Man was lucky I didn't have a gun or knife. Just hung on to them and the man was lucky because I couldn't see nothing but my two children right then. I hadn't lied to Miss Laura. I could easy kill him where he stood.

Couldn't stop hugging them. Picked them both up and walked away with them and the man he put his hand on me, was going to stop me, but Miss Laura she saw what was happening and came over.

"Are these your children?" she whispered in my ear soft, and I nodded.

"I'll handle this."

"He touches them again I'll gut him like a hog." I was crying but felt cold inside.

"I said I'll handle it." She turned away and back to Chivington, all smiles and gushy. "William, *darling*, the most amusing thing has just happened. You simply *won't* believe it. I hired these two girls back in Georgia, and it seems that one of them had lost her children . . ."

And off she went, took Chivington with her,

and I took Tyler and little Delie into my room. Couldn't put them down. Couldn't stop holding them, hugging them.

"Mammy, why are you here?" Tyler asked.

"Come looking for the two of you and this nice lady helped me. I knew you'd come to New Orleans with that man—did he hurt you?"

Tyler shook his head. "No. He just got us from that man who took us from you. I guess he paid for us. He brought us here and has been feeding us good and taking care of us all right 'cept he isn't you. I got to missing you something bad."

"Me too." Little Delie she held my arm like a harness clamp. "Missed you more every day."

"You're with me now. We'll never be apart again."

"Who is that?" Tyler he saw Tyler Two sleeping on Lucy's couch.

"That's a little boy we found back in the war. His folks were killed and he can't talk."

"What's his name?"

"I called him Tyler Two—number two. You're Tyler One."

"But he's white—how'd you come on a white boy?"

"We just found him. Don't worry on him.

Miss Laura she's looking for a good home for him. Are you sure you're all right?"

He nodded and I hugged them again and the door popped open. Miss Laura she was there, smiling, and she closed the door in back of her.

"It's all right. I've got the silly fool thinking he's done a good thing, saving your children for you. God, men are so . . . so simple." She looked on the children. "They both look like you. Hello, young man, how are you? And your little girl?"

"I'm fine, miss. How are you?" Tyler One said. Delie just smiled.

"Well, I'm fine too. But I have to get back to my party. You stay here, Sarny, we'll work around you."

"No. Let me put them down to sleep and then I'll come help."

They didn't want me to leave them and it 'bout made me cry all over looking on them but I shushed and shooed them and kissed them and told them I'd be right outside the door if they needed me. Put them to bed on the floor under a blanket with my smell on it. When they were asleep I kissed them one more time and went back out into the party.

Never saw so many people in one room. Four men had come with musical instruments and they were playing at the end by the piano but you couldn't hear much of it. Everybody had broken up into little groups and they were all drinking and talking and one would talk louder and that would make the next talk louder.

Just noise.

I worked my way through to the kitchen and helped Lucy who was about going crazy with it.

"My children are here," I said. "I've got them back."

She threw her arms around me. "Miss Laura she told me! I can't believe it—just walking in the door like that." She had tears in her eyes. "Lord, I'm happy for you, Sarny," Lucy said. "But now—get to handing things out. There's too many of them for me to keep up."

I grabbed a tray and we kept going back and forth and when the food ran out I started helping Bartlett carry drinks and before long everybody was so silly they didn't miss the food.

Went like that all night. Crazy. Just back and forth and Bartlett he would pour something in glasses and we would carry it out on trays and then come back for more. They drank whatever he poured. He'd run out of one and pour something else and they'd drink it and not notice anything had changed.

I checked on my babies time and again and they were sleeping soft, holding the blanket against their little faces. Then I'd go back to the crowd.

Crazy. Never saw folks so crazy before 'cept Waller and he was mean crazy. Would get so mad he would spit at the mouth like a hound slobbering.

This was different. Happy crazy. Men dancing with women, women dancing with women, men dancing with men. All laughing and screaming at each other over the noise.

One man, fat and red in the face, stood up on the table. I thought it would break but it was as stout as the man and he held up his glass and bellered like a bull, *"To the end of the war,"* and I thought must not be any rebels in *this* room; must not have been many rebels in New Orleans at all, leastways not real ones. He drank everything in his glass and everybody in the room drank and somebody yelled, *"Trust Laura to have the best end-of-the-war party anywhere!"* And they all drank to that.

Then another man climbed on the table and looked right at me and held his glass out and yelled, *"To the end of slavery!"* They all turned to me and drank to that and one of them, short man, looked like a frog and had a scar down his cheek Miss Laura she told me later was from a duel with a man who called him ugly to his face, he tried to pick me up and carry me around the room but I gave him a little tap on the head with an empty tray I was carrying and he put me down. Heavy old tray. I worried that he might go down but he didn't seem to notice it and the party went on.

Went on all night.

People just didn't want to leave. One of the women—tall woman, all legs but older than Lucy by a good ten years—sat at the piano just before dawn and started singing sad songs about the war. 'Bout boys that weren't coming home and laying buried in far fields, 'bout women dying of broken hearts. Everybody got quiet and then started in to crying and leaning on each other.

Still drinking. Never stopped drinking until, finally, when the sun was coming in the windows by the piano, finally somebody came to me for his coat and they started leaving. Sniffling, laughing, hugging Miss Laura and thanking her for the party, they came for their coats and left and each of them gave me a coin when I got their clothes.

"For your trouble," they'd say.

Every one of the men handed me money

and I put it in the pocket of my uniform dress and thanked them.

At last they were gone. Miss Laura she had some hair loose but I swear didn't look any the worse for it. Lucy she was sitting in a chair by the table sound asleep. Straight up and sound asleep. I was afraid to sit down for fear the same thing would happen to me.

"Well," Miss Laura said. "Wasn't that a party?"

"And I got my babies back."

"Yes. You got them back. Oh, Chivington wasn't as bad as we thought. He was passing the yard in his carriage and saw them in the pens and knew the war was moving south. He said he bought them to get them out before something bad could happen to them."

"Didn't try to find their mother, though, did he?"

"No. He didn't come looking for you. Still, he said he didn't hurt them and meant to raise them after a fashion. He's very rich and never married and wants to leave his money to somebody; or perhaps he was just bored. No matter, I believe in his way he would take good care of Tyler Two . . . if you agree." She looked around the room and sighed. "Quite a night!"

"I'll get to cleaning here in a minute."

"You'll do no such thing. We're all going to

sleep before we do another thing—ahh, Bartlett, how thoughtful."

Bartlett he had come out of the kitchen with another bottle and a tray with four glasses. It was some of that cordial and he poured each glass half full and handed them to us. Woke Lucy up and handed her one too but she set it down and went back to sleep.

"To the end of the war," Miss Laura said, "and the end of slavery but mostly to Sarny's babies coming home."

Drank to that and then went into my room and laid down next to little Delie and Tyler and closed my eyes.

Happiest day of my life.

FOURTEEN

Settled in.

Pretty soon it was like I'd always been there.
Before long I was marketing as good as Bartlett—or near as good—and had learned to
cook all the fancy things and knew what Miss
Laura she liked for different times.

Same breakfast every morning. One egg,
boiled soft on the inside, white part hard, two
pieces of toast and thick black coffee with
chicory in it when she got up. Though she
didn't get up sometimes until middle of the
day, 'specially had she been entertaining.

Sometimes a second meal in the afternoon.
Little fruit and cheese with vegetable. Usually
a dinner—I called it supper—did she have
company in the evening. Some of those dinners would break the table. Leg of lamb,
whole suckling pig, ten-pound beef roast,
pheasants or ducks, sweet potatoes, turnips,
bowls of candy. Sometimes be just two of them
and they'd only eat a speck and then we'd

have leftovers for days. I never ate so well in my life before or after as picking up from Miss Laura's dinners.

And the guests sometimes handed me a dollar, when I got their coats. Miss Laura she said these were tips. I always shared the money with Lucy and Bartlett but even so it come near doubling my wage.

Forty dollars a month and nothing to spend it on. I put it all in a sock in my room and slept with it under my head. Just in case, I thought—felt good having that money there. Knew did it all stop I had enough to get off somewhere and start over.

The children they came along better than I could hope. Miss Laura she had one more room which she gave to Lucy for her own self and that left me my room with the children. I found two small beds for three dollars at the market and made them up for little Delie and Tyler and set them to learning right away. Tyler Two he moved to Chivington's.

I started in to learning right off my own self. Miss Laura she gave me some of her own books and she found some books for children called primers and I used them for Tyler and little Delie and before too many weeks had passed I had them reading at a good rate. Tyler he was some slower than little Delie and he'd frown and make the words sound out loud sometimes when he read but he started getting it and pretty soon read without even moving his lips.

My own self I couldn't believe how much there was to learn. Thought just in living I'd learned such a load my head couldn't hold it all. Miss Laura she alone taught me so much I was near to bursting with it, and Bartlett, and guests who came and sometimes talked when I could hear them—I just kept learning. But when I got inside the books she brought me! Oh my, oh my Lord.

Started learning on the world. It went everywhere, went on forever. Read about other places, other times, other people. Read things made me laugh and some made me cry. Read on great men and some so downright bad they made Waller look good. Read every night when I could, when I didn't have to work, sitting by the milk-glass lamp with the book while my babies slept. Sometimes read sitting in the bathtub and thought once God, not swearing but praying, God if you could just let Delie see me now sitting in bubbles and hot water reading.

One day Miss Laura she gave me a book by a man named Shakespeare. Book was a play, called *Hamlet,* and I set to reading it. Hard at first, kind of music I couldn't make in my head right off but then I pushed at it and one night it all went into my brain and I started to see it. Couldn't believe it. Sitting alone with the lamp and my babies sleeping, reading this man Miss Laura said had been dead hundreds of years. I couldn't believe it was just him. He was so good, made words so good I thought it must have come from God in some way. Couldn't be a man write like that just his own self. Had to come from God and I started in to reading the Bible while I read on *Hamlet*, trying to see was it all in the Bible some place, was it all in God's word but it wasn't. It was Shakespeare.

Thought, thank you. Sitting there just thought thank you. To Nightjohn for bringing me reading, for Miss Laura for bringing me the book and mostly to Shakespeare for writing such a thing.

More to it. Few days later I was talking on Shakespeare to Miss Laura and she told me he had written other plays, many plays, and she would get them for me and when she did I found they were all like that first one. All good. All so good they must have come from more than a man.

Read after that all the time. Sometimes carried a book with me to the market. Miss Laura she gave us one day a week off and I'd take the children down by the river and sit in the grass in the sun with them and read Shakespeare out loud to them while they watched the big paddle wheelers going by on their way up the river.

Later Tyler he told me, later when he was a man and doing man things, studying on being a doctor, later than that when he was married and giving me grandchildren, that later he told me once he thought the finest thing that ever happened to him was sitting by the river having me read Shakespeare on a summer day.

Finest thing.

Lucy got to be more colty every day and there came a time when Miss Laura she saw one of the guests looking at Lucy the wrong way. Lucy she just couldn't help it. You could have put her in gunnysacks and Lucy she would have shown through some way. In her eyes, her smile.

"We have got to get her married," Miss Laura said one morning when I brought her breakfast. "Soon."

"Yes ma'am." She'd have me bring two cups and sit and have coffee while she ate breakfast and we planned the day. Loved that coffee in the morning. Would put two spoons of sugar in it and thick cream and it just made my whole day. Can still smell the chicory in it. Get Lucy married. "I thought that back on the plantation and on the road coming here—she pulls them in like flies to honey."

"Well, we're not without resources." She took a bite of toast. Chewed it with small bites. For such a big woman in her mind, she was dainty in her manner. "I will look for a suitable husband for her."

Only time I saw Miss Laura fail.

Oh, she found a husband. Found a dozen of them. She put the word out that she was shopping for Lucy and we had to beat them off with sticks. Some were bad, some were good and some were better than good. One man he wore a twenty-dollar suit and had a derby and two houses and his own carriage. Plus didn't you look too close at his teeth he was fair to good looking.

But Lucy she had met a man in the market. Boy, really, not much older than her but she fell in love with him, or what she thought to be love, and she brought him home to meet us. Meet the family.

Carl. Had a last name—Jefferson. Carl Jefferson. Had been a slave and when freedom came he went to work carrying loads at the grain booth in the market. My own self I'd been spending some extra time at the market talking to Stanley. Just talking, mind, 'cept Stanley he wanted it to go some further. But I was all for just talk for a time. Wasn't going to hurry into anything until I saw how he was with Delie and Tyler, and besides, it wasn't like Martin. Didn't feel that same feeling when I saw him. Something nice but not the same. Didn't make my stomach flop.

Carl Jefferson. Nice boy. But just about as dumb as a field stone. I swear did his brain not do it for him he'd forget to take a breath.

So naturally Lucy she falls in love with this Carl. Don't even look at all the prospects Miss Laura found for her. Looks right past them to this Carl and they find a minister for a dollar who marries them and they take off. Clean away. Lucy she came and said to Miss Laura, "Carl and I are leaving."

I stood with my mouth open.

"Leaving?" Miss Laura was holding a glass of cordial and she set it down on the table carefully. "You're actually going away?"

"Yes ma'am. We're going up North to find work."

And blamed if they didn't. Left that day and 'bout two months later I got a letter from Lucy. They had found work at a meat-packing place in Chicago and Lucy she was with child and said she couldn't be happier. Funny edge to the letter though. Short sentences like she'd thought on them too much before writing them and I found later it wasn't all true. She was with child all right and Carl he had a job at the meat-packing place but he had found whiskey and liked it and was hitting her now and again. It went bad to worse and he beat her solid once and she left him and married again. This time got a good one name of Buddy and had a good life after that. Three children and they all grew and lived and she wrote to me every Christmas until one day her heart it quit, when she was about sixty, and that was the last I heard of her family. Too short to live, sixty. You don't really learn much on life until then and it's a shame not to get to use it.

Then one day Stanley and me we were down by the river sitting and he asked me to marry him. He'd asked before, maybe half a dozen times, and I put him off. Thought on it now though and nodded. "All right. But I want to talk to Miss Laura first."

Did it at breakfast while we were sitting drinking coffee planning the day.

"Miss Laura, Stanley he asked me to marry him and I'm going to do it."

She put her coffee down. Same as when Lucy had told her. "Does this mean you're leaving too?"

"No ma'am. I couldn't leave you even if I wanted to and I don't want to. I just don't want to do it unless you think I should."

"You would have to move in with Stanley. He wouldn't want to live here."

"Yes ma'am. I thought we would rent a small house down there by the river. I'd come here every morning and make breakfast and work late when you had a guest. Same as now. It ain't but a ten-minute walk to the river."

"I think"—she took a breath and smiled—"it's a wonderful idea. Do you want a big wedding?"

"No ma'am. I was married before and I don't want a fuss."

"Very well, but I'm very good at things like this."

"I know, ma'am. But I still want to keep it small. We'll just go to a preacher."

Miss Laura she nodded but she wouldn't let it go and when Stanley and I we married up she took the children and sent us by boat north up the river and back for five days by way of a honeymoon.

Never saw anything like that boat. We had to stay in the colored section but we had a room, our own, and I saw the other parts of the boat. There was a salon room as pretty as Miss Laura's, and just about as big. Lot of rich white men sitting there playing cards for stacks of money.

We just watched the river go by and had

meals cooked by a woman who worked on the back end of the boat just cooking for passengers. Grits and pork and cornmeal and honey and coffee in the morning so thick a spoon would 'bout stand in it. Made me think of being a little girl—some of the nice parts. Delie, praying and laughing all the time. Soft mornings with Martin. Stanley he made me think of Martin but they were different, both good in their way, and by the end of the boat ride it was like we'd been married forever.

We got back to find Miss Laura she had bought us a small house down on the river as a wedding present. Had two little bedrooms, one for us and one for the children and a small kitchen and a little parlor. Sweet little house. I painted the bedrooms soft white and the parlor a gentle tan and the kitchen white as clouds. There was some furniture there and we found more in a booth at the market and I had me a home.

Hadn't been a year and a half since I was a slave and I had me a home for my own self and hadn't it turned so sour it might have been my best memory.

FIFTEEN

The years seemed to blink past and for a long time things just got better.

Miss Laura she gave me a raise. Doubled me to forty dollars a month and Stanley he made close to thirty at the market and we didn't have anything to spend it on but lamp oil and the children. Didn't have to buy food because of what I brought home from Miss Laura's when she entertained.

And she entertained 'most all the time. Some of what she did I knew and understood and won't write on it. Don't care to. But parts of it I didn't. Sometimes single men would come but sometimes it would be men and women and they would sit and talk business all night and she would laugh and pour drinks for them and chat with them and they would leave.

I don't know how she made money on all this and we didn't talk about her work or money but she must have made more than most. She spent money like water on food and good wine and caviar and always paid in full each month. Once I saw her talking to three men and one of them said something about investing in a new business that was coming to town. Something about hatmaking. And she gave him an envelope with money in it so maybe that's how she did it. Helped to start businesses or loaned money.

We didn't talk on it so I didn't find out until later. Didn't matter. I had my work to do and my studies at home. I was getting to be fair at arithmetic and had Stanley reading 'bout as good as me. He never took to Shakespeare the way I did but he read the paper every night sitting in a chair by the oil lamp in the parlor while I studied at a desk in the corner with another lamp. Couldn't get enough. Like I was dying of thirst to know more all the time. Same for Tyler and little Delie, though they weren't such children anymore.

Tyler he was getting to where he looked at girls and little Delie she was starting to get legs on her. Didn't matter. They'd always be my babies and of an evening when I sat and read sometimes I'd read aloud and they got to thirsting after more like me. Tyler he was a serious boy, seemed to take time to think on things, and Delie she had a mind on her that set like a steel trap on ideas.

Stanley he watched me one night, reading to them, and he said, "You know, Sarny, you know so much you ought to teach other young ones."

"Me? A teacher? I guess *not* . . ."

"Think on it. You're so good at it you've got these sprites reading more than most grownups ever do. And they ain't sick of it yet. I hear talk at the market lots of people wish there was a colored school to get more young ones to reading. Why don't you start one?"

"Maybe you hadn't noticed—I've got me a full-time job."

"Just an hour now and then. Miss Laura she wouldn't grudge you that. And you have a day off."

"I like to sit by the river . . ."

He nodded. "And I like to sit with you. But an hour from your day off wouldn't be so bad."

Sat there smoking his pipe. He liked a corncob pipe in the evening after working all day. Would drink some herb tea and smoke his pipe and read the paper. Smell of twist cut tobacco filled the room. Tasted awful on his lips but smelled good in the room. Still smell that tobacco. Such a good man, my Stanley. Always good.

So I went to Miss Laura and she surprised me by being against it.

"I think it's a bad idea."

"I won't miss any work."

"It's not that. I know how good you are. It's just that there are people who still haven't lost the war. There are many who do not want us colored to learn reading and writing—do not want us better than we were. I'm afraid if you start a school you will set yourself up to be noticed, and the people who notice you will be bad people, Sarny."

"I know about them. Night riders, white-sheet riders."

"Sarny, they're hurting people. Shooting and stringing people up. Anybody they think is getting out ahead they notice and they might do bad things to you."

I thought on it, then shook my head. "Listen to you. Wasn't that long ago I was in the quarters and man could sell me or whatever. Then there was the war and people died and set us free. We can't turn that around now and let a little thing like fear put us back. Got to keep going."

She studied on me for a long time. Must have been a minute and then she nodded slow, head up once, down once. "There can be no other way for you." She sighed. "Well, that's it then. I'll do all I can to help you."

And she did. Found an old small house down in the section by the river and bought it flat out to make a school. Stanley and the children and me we spent our spare time fixing on it and cleaning it up and painting it. Found some chairs and then Miss Laura she bought a bunch of old small tables for desks and a blackboard and chalk. Don't know where she found all the makings for a school but she did. Wagon would come with tables, wagon would come with blackboard, wagon would come with chairs. Miss Laura she just knew how to get things done. And I set to work teaching.

Taught three days a week, one hour in the evening each day, and two hours on Monday, my day off.

At first nobody came. Then Stanley he told it around the market that we were ready and after that we didn't have the room. Tyler and little Delie they helped and Stanley when he could but even so sometimes I thought we had started a flood we couldn't stop.

Near everybody wanted to learn to read. Wasn't just children, neither. 'Bout the second week I came to teach after working at Miss Laura's and there was a crowd of people waiting by the door and I thought, wonder what they want, all standing there. Must have been twenty or thirty of them.

Wanted to learn.

So I set in to teaching. Didn't know how at

first but Miss Laura she found me some books on it and I had helped Nightjohn back on the plantation and remembered on that.

Taught them letters. Taught them to make the sound and the letter at the same time and when some got to getting it faster than others I did the same as Nightjohn with me and turned them to teaching each other.

Same with numbers. Got one or two to working them right and they went to helping others and pretty soon 'most everybody could do sums and even fractions. Funny sight. Little sprite no more than eight years old teaching sums to a man had to be over forty. Just as natural as daylight.

They called it Sarny's Riverside School and somebody even painted the name over the door in gold letters. Did it when I wasn't there and I never found out who but it looked fine in the afternoon sun. Little school with my name on it.

No trouble seemed to come. Months went by and coming on a year and the school it was getting so big I was talking to Miss Laura about using canvas to make a tent nearby to hold the extra.

Then it burned down. Nobody hurt but one night the school it burned. No reason at first and I thought somebody left a lamp on and it tipped over and the oil caught the house. But nobody owned up to it and people found wood for a frame and canvas and we made a new school in not much over a week. Not as nice as the first one but it kept the weather out and we found new tables and a blackboard and set to teaching again.

Then I was walking back one night from Miss Laura's and two white men they stopped me in a dark place away from any lights. One of them held a lantern up to my face.

"You the one teaching at the colored school?" Only he didn't say colored. Used the other word. I don't use it, ever—just gives them more. Hate to give them more.

I didn't say anything but the other man he swore and said, "Yeah, this is the one. I've seen her before."

"You people aren't supposed to be reading." He hit me in the shoulder. Not hard. I've been hit harder by kittens. But he hit me. I thought on killing him but I didn't have a knife or club. I'd start carrying one though. Carry a butcher knife in a bag. They do this again they wouldn't be going home. Won't have anybody lay a hand on me. "We burned you once, and if you don't shut it down we'll burn you again. And maybe we'll throw you in the fire when we do it. You understand?"

Still didn't talk. Thinking, well, it wasn't a lamp tipping over. Thinking Miss Laura she was right—some don't want us better. Rather keep us down.

The same man he hit me on the shoulder again, a little harder, then they went away into the dark and I walked home. I was some scared but I didn't dare tell Stanley or the children because Stanley he'd go out and try to find them and whip up on them.

Told Miss Laura though and she nodded.

"I expected it before this. Are you going to shut the school down?"

I stared at her. "What do you think?"

"I think," she said, letting her breath out slowly, "that you're going to get in trouble."

"Can't stop teaching, can I? Without them winning?"

"No, I think not."

"Can't let them win."

"No."

"They burn it down and we'll build another."

"Yes."

"And another."

"I know all that but, Sarny, they might do worse than that. These men are entirely capable of violence. They might kill you."

"I take some killing," I said. "More than most."

"How did I know you'd say that?" She shook her head. "Well, as I said before, I'll help all I can but I cannot control what those men do. I've tried but I simply I don't have any contacts who can reach them."

"There's so many of us now in the school, children and grown-up, that they wouldn't dare do anything to one of us. We'll be all right."

"I know you think that, but I fear for you, Sarny. I fear for you."

Went back to the school and kept teaching and it kept growing and nobody came to burn it. Months went by, fall to spring and spring to summer, and nobody came to bother and I told Miss Laura one morning while we were having coffee in her room, "It's like I said— we're too many for them to keep coming at us."

She didn't say anything but didn't nod either and I knew she didn't agree with me and we went ahead and planned on a party she was going to have that night for a senator and some of his friends.

"I need the party to go especially well," she said. "The senator is working on a bill governing shipping on the Mississippi. I have some interests there and need him in a good frame of mind."

So we set the party up right. Best food, best wine and best music and I didn't head home until dawn the next morning, just first light and happened to walk past the school when three men they came running out of it. All white men. Not hiding their faces. Saw smoke come up from the back of the tent-school and I ran to stop it but it was too late. They must have put lamp oil on the canvas because it went so fast I near didn't get out my own self. Didn't have time to save anything but a handful of pencils.

But I saw the men and knew one of them. Name of Haggerty. Ugly man, walked with a limp from a horse breaking his leg years before. He had a booth in the market where he sold leather goods. Harness leather.

Should have kept my mouth shut. Knew it later and wish to God I had but I went home and Stanley he was just getting ready to go to work and I swore and told him.

"They burned the school. I saw them. One of them was that Haggerty from the leather booth."

"You're sure?"

"I saw him clear as light."

"Does he know you saw him?"

"I suppose so. He saw me."

"Well then I 'spect I'll have a talk with him."

He was gone before I could stop him. Wasn't thinking right because I hadn't slept all night and I had an anger on me that burned like a sore. Kept me from thinking straight and I didn't chew on what I'd done for a full ten minutes.

Stanley he was slow to anger but when he did it was a fright. Only saw it once when he got mad at a mule that somebody left tied near the fish booth. Mule kept getting into things, making messes, and Stanley he went to move the mule and it wouldn't move. Gentle man, Stanley, slow and soft and gentle, kept pulling on the mule and it wouldn't come and the mule it finally bit him. Looked like a snake—that fast it just out and bit him and he said real soft, "Damn mule," and hit it once, right between the eyes, and that mule went down like it had been shot with one of those wheel guns from the war.

Now he was going to go "talk" to Haggerty about burning the school. Wouldn't be a problem except for Stanley getting his anger up.

And Haggerty he was white.

There was freedom but it wasn't anywhere near clean yet. Some places the colored couldn't use and some places they weren't allowed to be and some things they weren't supposed to do.

Like hitting a white man. Even when they deserved it hitting a white man was dangerous because it scared other white people who thought on how bad they'd been to black people in the past and were worried on the black people getting it back. And Miss Laura she said it, "My dear Sarny, there are very few things more dangerous than a scared white person, because they have all the guns."

I should never have told on who I saw and I knew it and ran after Stanley hoping to catch him before he got to the market but I was too late. He had a good ten minutes on me and the bad luck held because Haggerty he was there in his booth.

People told me later. Stanley he walked up and said, "My wife she saw you set fire to the school this morning."

"Your wife is lying."

"My wife she don't lie."

Then they say Haggerty he pushed Stanley away from his booth and called him names and Stanley he didn't say anything but his eyes got a storm in them and he started in to hitting Haggerty. Haggerty was a no-count anyway, not much on muscle, and once Stanley he started he couldn't stop and beat him down and then set in to kicking him. It was all over in five minutes.

He came close to killing Haggerty and then he walked back to the fish booth and I came. Saw him there sucking his knuckles and went over to where everybody was looking down at Haggerty on the ground in front of his booth and I thought, please don't be dead, please don't be dead.

He wasn't but it didn't matter and I knew it. I went to the booth and took Stanley over to the side. "You have to run."

"Run? Why?"

"You beat a white man down and other white men are going to be mad."

"It will be all right, Sarny. He was just trash. Even white folks know it. They won't bother me and even did they want to I ain't running. We don't run anymore."

"I have money. A lot of money. You take some and head up north to Chicago. The children and I will follow. Just go. Please."

"I ain't running."

Was like a wall, standing there. I couldn't get him loose no matter what and I knew the more I tried the more stubborn he would get. Couldn't push a wall.

"Now you go home. I've got work to do and I'll be along presently." He put his hand on my arm. "Head on home now. I'll be along after work."

Wasn't anything for it but to go and I did. Had the day off because of the party the night before and I spent the day fretting but he came home that evening and we had supper and I thought he was right. Haggerty he was trash and even the whites knew it.

I was wrong.

They came about middle of the night. I had been so tired I was in dead sleep and didn't wake up until I felt Stanley moving against me to get up.

"What's the matter?" Thinking on the children, though they were 'most grown now. Always thinking on them.

"Somebody out front, pounding on the door."

Cold then, cold cut right through me. "Don't go. Let them pound."

"Got to see who it is. Might be a neighbor on fire."

"Don't . . ."

But he was gone. I tumbled out and followed him and he opened the door just as I came. Men on horses wearing white robes, hoods, some carrying torches. Eight, ten, dozen men on horses and as soon as Stanley opened the door a man hidden to the side dropped a rope over his neck. Rope was tied to one of the horses and the rider he turned and stuck spurs to the horse and took off. Snapped Stanley off his feet and dragged him on out by the neck.

I screamed and ran out but another man hit

me in the back of the head with something hard and I saw a bright light in my brain and went down. Didn't pass out but I couldn't move, couldn't make my own self get up. Hung like that on my hands and knees, head spinning. Thought on the children. Had to get up and help the children but the men they didn't bother the children. Didn't bother me anymore. Had what they wanted and they turned and rode off dragging Stanley by the neck.

In a few minutes I could stand. Tyler he was there helping me and little Delie, she standing there crying, eyes wide. Tyler he just looked mad.

"Bastards," he said.

"Don't swear." Couldn't help myself. Though I thought the bad word I didn't say it. "Swearing won't help. I have to go now, help me to go."

"Go?"

"Have to find where they took Stanley. Get me to walking right so I can go. Then you and little Delie stay here. I'll be back after I fetch Stanley."

"Why, they could take him anywhere."

"Then that's where I'll go. Get me to walking now."

Tyler he helped me until I was steady and then he wouldn't go back but stayed with me and after a time I was glad because I leaned on him.

They didn't take Stanley far. Just back to the market. They had thrown the rope over the poles that held the big sign at the gate into the market and pulled him up and he was hanging there dead. I 'spect he was dead before he was out of the yard with a broken neck but something in me hadn't wanted to believe it. Wanted to think he was still alive. But I knew it now and started in to crying while Tyler he helped me to untie the rope and get him down. They had some trash note written and pinned to his shirt and I tore it off and threw it away.

My poor Stanley, I thought. My poor, poor Stanley. Just wanted to be a man and look what they did to you. He was scuffed up from the dragging and I tried to wipe him off with the hem of my sleeping dress.

People started to come and they helped Tyler and me carry him home. Took a door from one of the stalls and used it to carry him and I cried until I thought my heart would break in two. Couldn't think of anything but poor Stanley, my poor dear Stanley.

SIXTEEN

Miss Laura she took care of everything. I couldn't make my brain work. All I knew was Stanley he was dead and it was my fault and I couldn't get my thinking past that.

Miss Laura she set the funeral and bought the coffin and found the minister and the hearse and the above-ground burial vault. They can't bury them in the ground because the water is too high. And I walked behind the coffin with Tyler and little Delie.

Couldn't think on anything. Minister he said some nice things about Stanley and there must have been two hundred people show up, almost all black but some white too.

"Stanley was well liked," the minister said. "If it is the measure of a man that God will like him as his neighbors do, then Stanley will be with our heavenly Father waiting for us. . . ."

Later at Miss Laura's I thought on quitting and told her so.

"No. You won't. Not now." And she had such a fire in her eye that it scared me. "Before all this you might have quit, but now you can't stop the school."

"But they're still there. That Haggerty he's still around, all of them are. They'll just come back, they'll just keep coming back and burning it down."

"We'll do it differently. We'll move around. Not give them a place to burn. But you can't stop now, not after what they've done. As to Haggerty, he won't be there long."

"What do you mean?"

"Even though there were other men involved, he was clearly responsible for Stanley's death. We'll have him arrested and punished for it."

"You mean the police?"

"Of course. It's a lynching—a murder. He's a criminal and must be punished."

"The police don't help us—"

"You forget who I am. Among other things I am a very close friend of the chief of police, and most of the judges. I think we won't be seeing much of Haggerty for a time."

Was as good as her word. I don't know what she had on men, what kind of hold, but the police they came to the market and arrested Haggerty right in front of everybody and took him to jail. Gave him a trial and had it fixed some way because the jury they came back with guilty for manslaughter and he went to prison. Whole thing didn't take but two weeks.

Wasn't as good as hanging him and it didn't bring Stanley back but it was something and after it was over Miss Laura she had a party for the judge and the attorneys for both sides and I helped Bartlett to serve. I knew who they were but they didn't know me and Miss Laura she didn't tell them I was Stanley's wife until after they'd had some to drink. Then she introduced me, told them I was Stanley's widow and that they had done a wonderful job of "upholding justice."

They all puffed up and clapped for me and then went right back to drinking and watching Miss Laura talk and move. When she was there men couldn't see much else and I worked until the party was over and then went home and for a week slept in the same room as little Delie and Tyler. Just couldn't be alone.

There for a space, time didn't matter. I know it passed and I know I lived and I know we did things but I can't remember on them. Everything was in a blue fog and I didn't care for much.

The school took care of itself. Enough knew

how to read and figure numbers that they could pass it on and they went to people's homes to hold class. Went to different places each week, sometimes more than one at the same time, and just kept it going like Miss Laura said, moving it around. I didn't have much to do with it and no matter what they did they couldn't stop it now. Delie cried some and grieved after Stanley but not as bad as Tyler. It like to broke him at first and then made him hard, like he had a place inside where he could never be hurt again.

Worked at Miss Laura's, went home, back to work, but everything seemed flat and it must have been eight months or more like that. Just living, not caring much. One morning I went to Miss Laura's and brought her coffee and breakfast and her face it was all gray. Only color to match it. Just gray.

"What's the matter?"

"I'm not feeling well. Not well at all. Would you send Bartlett for Dr. Hyram, please? And you can take the breakfast away. I won't be eating this morning. I'm sorry for the bother."

Bartlett must have run all the way because the doctor was there in fifteen minutes. I had never, not once, seen Miss Laura sick. Even her monthlies didn't seem to bother her. For her to send for a doctor I knew it was bad and he was in her bedroom a long time. When he came out he looked at me. "She wants you." And I thought, didn't look good. Voice too short. Face too serious. *She wants you.*

I went in and she was sitting up in bed. Face still gray, voice weak. Tired but more, sunken. Her voice had gone down inside her.

"Sarny, I need you to do more than you're accustomed to doing for a time."

"What's the matter?"

"My heart has failed. The doctor says I am going to die."

No. Didn't say it but thought it hard. No. You can't die. You can't. I won't let you. "You're too young to have a bad heart."

"I am fifty-one years old." She sighed, spoke even weaker. "Apparently that is old enough. The doctor assured me there is no hope."

She couldn't be that old. I thought maybe thirty and eight. Less. I started in crying. Been crying a lot lately and this just made it worse. "Can't be. You were just fine yesterday. You can't be fine one day and dying the next. Has to be some time there. More time. We need more time."

"Sarny, I need you to be strong. There is a lot that needs doing, and there isn't much time. I must depend on you to do it."

"How long does the doctor say?"

She took a breath. "Days. Not over a week. And there is much to do."

"Bartlett can help."

"Bartlett won't be able to handle this. He will fall apart. You have always been the strong one, and I need your strength now. Will you help me?"

"Anything." Meant it too. Would have died for this woman. Right now, instead of her I'd die. Take me, not her. "Just tell me what to do."

"First, we must discuss business. I do not have a family, and I have amassed a considerable sum. I wish to leave some of it to Bartlett so he'll be comfortable the remainder of his life. The rest I'm leaving to you."

"Me? I've got my own money. More than I'll ever need."

"We will do as I say." Strength there. Weak voice but strong inside and I shut my mouth.

"Good. Now, get paper and a pen and I will tell you whom to contact. You must get busy right away. Bartlett can run errands for you, take messages. Oh, let's not tell him just yet, all right? Now get the paper."

I went to the table in the corner and took a pen and dipped it in the ink. "Ready."

She listed names of men and names of companies, three different lawyers to contact and bring immediately, and I wrote as fast as I could, putting the notes in envelopes and addressing them by name when they were done. Sometimes she had to stop so I'd catch up but then we'd go again. After an hour she stopped. "All right, get Bartlett busy and let me rest for a few minutes. I'd like a cup of beef broth if you have some extract. And some hot tea."

I sent Bartlett off on the errands without telling him about Miss Laura. He didn't ask about the doctor, and the errands just seemed normal to him and he left. Made a tray up with flowers stolen from the courtyard below, hot tea and beef broth both and some cold vegetable soup in case she wanted a bit more.

She was sleeping when I came back in the room and I started to close the door but her eyes opened. "Didn't mean to wake you."

"I will get more sleep than I want soon enough. Now, on to the next thing. My final party."

"You're going to have a party feeling like this?"

"Not exactly. I mean my funeral. I want it to be a wake. I want to be there and I want to be wearing that deep purple dress that makes my hair look so nice. You tell the undertaker to dress me in that. And not too much makeup—I hate that pancake-batter look they often do on bodies."

I was writing again. Didn't want to miss anything, do anything wrong.

"You call Williams Mortuary for the body."

Couldn't believe she's talking about her own self that way. Just as calm and cool as the river. The body. Not me, or I, but the body.

"I want that Clarion orchestra to play music at the party, and I want to be near the piano with the top half of the coffin open." She took a sip of the broth. "They say the dead can still hear music for a time, and I want to see if that's so. Now, to the guest list . . ."

"How are you going to know if they come?" Couldn't help it. Thought of just the three of us sitting alone, nobody there.

"Oh, they'll come, don't worry. Most of them owe me money. They'll owe you now. They'll want to keep me and, hence, you happy. They'll all come."

She listed over forty names. All men. Some I knew, most I knew, some I did not.

"Bartlett has all their addresses. Just tell him that we're having a party."

"What day?" Hated to ask but had to say something.

"Ahh yes, there is that, isn't there?" She frowned. "It's so hard to know. Let's make it a week from today, and if it happens sooner . . ."

Don't say it, I thought. Don't talk about saving the body for the party. Can't stand that. Just don't talk on it.

"Make it a week," she said again. "That should do it. Oh, I want an old-fashioned New Orleans funeral. I want a band in front of a parade procession leading me to the cemetery and playing while I am interred. All right?"

"Whatever you want, that's what it will be."

"Good. Now get started while I consider the menu for the party. Oh, and you may want to run home and tell little Delie and Tyler you'll need to sleep here for a time. If that's all right."

"I'll send Bartlett." Didn't say it but I didn't want to leave. "He can tell them I have to work."

We didn't have long to wait before the lawyers started coming. All three came at the same time and I had to wait while she spoke to them one at a time in her bedroom. They all said they were sad and I think they meant it. One of them cried. The third one she talked to was the man that did her will. Man name of Brune. She had already put me in it without telling me so there wasn't anything to change but she wanted to make certain Bartlett was settled right.

"He will receive one hundred dollars a month for life," Brune told her. I thought, a hundred a month. Twice what a man made working. Almost three times. Must have more money than me and I had a pile. What with not spending wages and tips I'd saved exactly two thousand four hundred and nine dollars and sixty-five cents. Enough to live for six, seven years without working should I get old. Couldn't think on more money than that. What would you do with it?

She rested for an hour when the lawyers were done and by the end of that day 'most everything was ready. I brought my blanket in and put it on the floor that night and started to sleep there but she stopped me.

"Please, Sarny, sleep on the bed, will you? Next to me? I have some fear . . ."

So I did and was next to her just at dawn the next morning when she passed. I was awake, thinking on coffee and breakfast, wondering should I do it, just lying still next to her hearing her breathe, and I looked over in the weak light coming through the window. Sun wasn't up yet but starting to get close and her eyes were open and she was looking at me and she took my hand and said, "Oh, Sarny, I did so like beautiful things."

And she died. Closed her eyes and her breathing stopped and I thought, no, God, not yet. But He took her and I thought bad on Him for a minute, but He still took her.

Felt like I'd lost another Delie, another

Martin, another Stanley. Thought my heart was already broken from the others but it wasn't. Broke again, just broke and I laid there crying next to her, holding her still hand, smelling the lilac in her hair, wishing I hadn't had to see so damn much misery. Feeling some sorry for my own self and wishing I could slide time backwards and have it not happen.

Didn't matter.

He took her anyway.

SEVENTEEN

Went just like she planned. Tyler and little Delie they had to help me with the wake and the funeral because Bartlett he fell apart just like Miss Laura said. Just sat in the corner of the kitchen crying softly, looking out the small window. Nothing to see but the building next door but he sat there a whole day and would have stayed longer 'cept that I took a bottle of cordial and a glass and put him in his room and made him drink it. The whole bottle.

He slept then but still wasn't good for much and during the funeral parade out to the cemetery we had to give him a ride in a carriage because he couldn't walk. Just kept crying and hanging on the hearse and falling down. He loved Miss Laura so much that he almost died himself. When the funeral was over he took to his bed and didn't get up for almost a week and I think would have passed 'cept that I brought him soup and soft bread and made him eat.

Miss Laura she had her burial vault picked. Didn't surprise me 'cept that I thought she was so young and it didn't seem a young person would think on death. 'Course she wasn't that young after all.

A week after the wake and funeral Brune he came to call. Had a case full of papers and folders and set them all on the table. We were still in Miss Laura's. She didn't own it but the rent was paid for a year and I slept at home but kept it up for Bartlett. He was coming along better but still couldn't think straight. Never saw grief that deep.

Brune he put on small spectacles and coughed to clear his throat and looked on Bartlett and told him what Miss Laura she had done for him. Bartlett set off crying again, moaning, and I helped him to his room and came back out to the table. Little Delie and Tyler they were there and Brune he asked them to leave.

"They can stay," I said. "They're my children."

He nodded. "I know. But Laura wished for you to hear some of this alone. I'm sorry, but those are her instructions."

"We'll go back to the house," Tyler said. "We can come back later."

Brune he waited until they were gone, then cleared his throat again and pushed the spec-

171

tacles up his nose. Red face. Red nose. White and red. Saw those things and couldn't help thinking on them though they had nothing to do with what we were doing.

"Sarny, you are now a very wealthy woman."

I nodded. "I know. I've been saving for years. It adds up."

"I mean the estate. I'm not sure you understand, but Miss Laura left you everything."

I nodded again. "I know. She told me before she passed over." Couldn't say died, couldn't think it. "But there isn't much of an estate. She rented this place and I don't know that she owns much else."

"She owns—*you* own"—he took out some papers—"four rental properties here in New Orleans, five rental properties in St. Louis, half interest in two riverboats, one-quarter interest in a bank here in New Orleans, a substantial number of shares in different businesses. She was very shrewd and all the shares are in Northern companies. I think she knew the South would lose the war and didn't wish to go down with them. And she owns quite a large amount of land situated here and there—some seven thousand acres." He took a breath. "She also left money in gold in approximately the amount of eighty-five thousand dollars. Add to this the fact that all the income properties and land bring in an added approximately forty-seven thousand dollars a year and, as I said, you are a very wealthy woman."

Just sat, trying to think. Couldn't. So much I couldn't even think on it, couldn't take a guess. "But . . ."

He smiled. "She said you would have trouble believing it. She instructed me to advise you until you wish me to stop."

"But . . ."

"Don't worry. I've already been paid for whatever I do for you. I would have done it for nothing. I thought very much of Laura and on several occasions asked her to marry me. I don't know how I'll handle her loss. . . ." All in the same tone. Businesslike, straight out, but I could see his eyes were misting up and knew he meant it.

"But what do I *do* with it all?"

Was all I could think to say.

Went to St. Louis.

Not right away. I had to stay in New Orleans near a year just to figure things out. Brune he worked with me as he said and I brought Tyler and little Delie into it so they could help me and they did fine. Little Delie she got to colting—she was eighteen—but she was more like me than Lucy and kept her head to business even when the other parts wanted to take the bit and run.

She brought home a man name of Isaac and wanted to marry him but wouldn't without my say-so. I talked to Isaac for a spell and he seemed better than most, had a good head on his shoulders and was working at the market steady, so I gave a nod.

They married but little Delie she kept her head for business and I was glad because Tyler he wanted to leave and go to school to be a doctor. He went off and pretty soon little Delie she was running things as well as I could and I went to St. Louis to see the properties up there.

Took the steamship *Henshaw* up the river. Had to ride in the colored section again but I rented a room. Tiny little thing and cost more than I wanted to spend but I like my privacy and what with stopping and starting and finding firewood for the boilers we were three weeks getting up to St. Louis and I was glad to have a room.

Passed my fortieth birthday on the river. I wasn't sure of my birth date but knew it close so I made it June ninth because I like the first part of June—soft summer nights, early summer birds and bugs singing. Had a cup of sassafras tea with my grits for a birthday party and missed Tyler and little Delie. They had their own lives and I thought on all that had gone, sitting there on the river, the paddle wheel churning as the riverbanks slid past like they were greased.

St. Louis it was a sick place. Never saw so many bodies coming and going without a war. Some kind of influenza was there and the whole city smelled of mud and vomit and death. Saw to things and then found a boat heading south and took it. Wasn't there a week and wished I hadn't come. The properties were taking care of themselves and I couldn't stand the smell or the crowds. Everybody not dead was hurrying to get somewhere. Too fast and not in a friendly way, like down South. Everybody edgy.

Back in New Orleans it was slower and I stayed there a year just doing business but felt bad, even though Delie she had a new baby name Samuel. Couldn't figure why I felt bad but little Delie she told me one morning. We had taken to having coffee of a morning like I had done with Miss Laura. Little Sam he sucked on a sugar sock and we sipped our black coffee and little Delie said, "You need something to do."

"I've got plenty to do. Money coming in, money going out—it all takes something."

"I can do all that. You need to work with people again. You need to teach."

And she was right. Knew it when she said it. Dead right. Wanted to be teaching and after that day I thought on it. There wasn't a need in New Orleans anymore. People learning, teaching each other. Those that wanted to learn could.

Had to go somewhere else and I couldn't see it until Tyler he told me. He was home from school up North and he had a friend going west.

"A lot of black people are going to Texas," he said. "There's work out there and places to live."

And that's how I came to be in Texas.

Left New Orleans and headed west by train and coach. Took three dresses and a box full of writing tablets and pencils and two more boxes full of books and stopped at the first town in Texas where there were black people.

Cruller, Texas.

Mostly cowboys and I had to laugh later when I saw my first movie about the West and all the white cowboys. Most of the cowboys I saw were black men. Boys, not men. Just boys. Headed out there to find those wild cattle and drive them north to railheads. Old joke said a cowboy was a man with a ten-dollar horse and a forty-dollar saddle. I saw them with no saddles and some with no horses. Running on foot into thick mesquite to rope a longhorn and drag it down. Wild as the cattle they caught.

But they had to learn too. They had wives and young ones and they all had to learn. Started a school in Cruller and in a year or so when some could teach others I moved on to the next town.

Beaufort. Same thing. Little Delie she sent me enough of my money to buy a small house for three hundred dollars and I turned it into a school and when one could teach another I moved on again.

Did that my whole lifelong life.

Did that until I was near eighty years old and had started maybe twenty schools. So many schools and so many faces looking up I couldn't remember them.

Did that until little Delie she was an old woman her own self with grandchildren and I had great-grandchildren and Tyler he was an old man and then he passed on and I had to go back and bury him.

Hard to do. Bury your own children. Hardest thing to do. They're meant to live longer than you. Your children. Tyler he had a good life. Too short, but good. He was a doctor for over thirty years and had a good practice, good wife, three good children, but it's hard to bury your young ones just the same.

Little Delie she made the money double

again several times until I doubt even she could count it. She kept sending me checks but I didn't need but forty dollars a month and money for books and five-cent tablets and penny pencils. Bit of chalk now and again. So most of the checks I just kept in a book and didn't cash them in.

Then came a day my body it didn't care what my brain told it to do. It was too tired to do more. Just too tired. So I found this home outside Dallas where the sun comes in the east window in the morning. Put myself in here. They don't let me drink coffee but I think on it, think on drinking coffee of a morning with Miss Laura and write these words on a tablet and wait.

Wait to go visit with Delie and Nightjohn and Miss Laura, and maybe see Martin again and Stanley and Tyler. And those four soldiers shot in the belly. I worry on them sometimes before sleep. Just boys never got to be men.

Wait to go visit my friends.

That's my whole life.

Afterword

As is *Nightjohn,* the first book about Sarny, this story is fiction, though everything in it is true in the sense that it happened to someone. And in that same sense all the fictional characters could in a way be considered real—or based on real people and real events—with the stipulation that events and characters have been moved around and renamed in the interest of story and flow.

I have tried to avoid the oft-used "big picture" concept, which I think is detrimental to many works of historical fiction. As an example, though Sarny witnessed what she thought were Civil War battles, in reality they were little more than skirmishes. A young woman newly freed from slavery would probably not be familiar with large events in the outside world and would see things from her own perspective and evaluate them with her own abilities.

I have written this book in this way in the hope that I will provide a more accurate and intimate look at what a life like Sarny's was really like.

> Gary Paulsen
> White Oaks, New Mexico
> January 1997